# THE STORY AND SCRIPTS BEHIND
# NO PLACE LIKE HOLMES

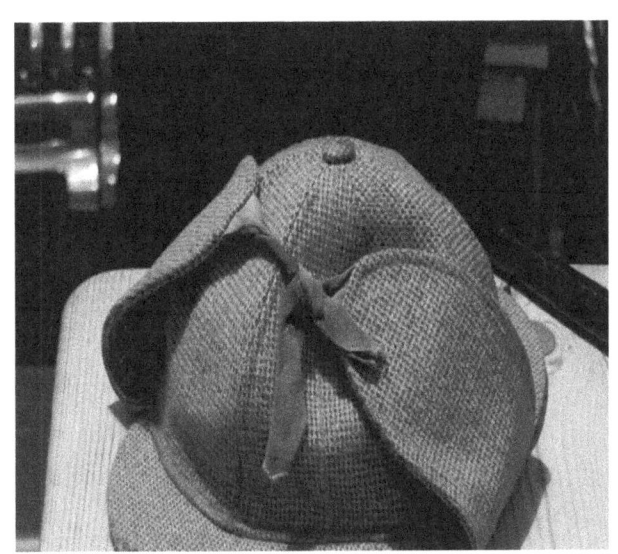

# BY
# ROSS
# K FOAD

Paperback ISBN  9781780924243
ePub ISBN  9781780924250
PDF ISBN  9781780924267

Published in the UK by MX Publishing
335 Princess Park Manor, Royal Drive,
London, N11 3GX
www.mxpublishing.co.uk
Cover design by www.staunch.com

# CONTENTS

## Foreword

Whether you refer to yourself as a Holmesian, a Sherlockian, or Fandom, I guarantee you one thing; *"No Place Like Holmes"* is a web-site that you **MUST** visit. How do I know this? Or why am I saying this, read on.

If one searches the internet for *WelcomeHolmes*, they would discover the web's largest Sherlock Holmes discussion group now in its 14th year. As part of that discussion group, under the nom of Straker, you would find numerous entries from Howard Ostrom who is described as an avid collector of thousands of DVDs of the Holmes saga, and who sends interesting links for current events and video finds he comes across. It was in that role of searching out interesting videos, that one day I came across on YouTube - Ross K. Reviews "The Lost Stories of Sherlock Holmes."

I found this review so cerebrate, while also being entertaining and informative at the same time, that I immediately searched out all the Ross K Reviews available, and relayed their links to the discussion group, with my highest possible recommendation. Who better than a group of Sherlockian scholars could appreciate a rating scale based on "Six Napoleons"!
I proceeded to follow the link supplied by the YouTube video to a web site known as "No Place Like Holmes." To my amazement I discovered that this young man, whom I knew only as Ross K, had also created "No Place Like Holmes," a web drama-comedy series based on Sir Arthur Conan Doyle's iconic characters Sherlock Holmes & Dr. Watson. I proceeded to watch all these videos, which featured as the major characters, Ross K. Foad as Sherlock Holmes, Mike Archer *(replacing an earlier Samuel Coe)* as Dr. Watson and Tamzin Dunstone as their housekeeper Miss Blake.

The premise of the narratives was that Holmes and Watson had been frozen in a time spell and were now living unruffled as Victorians, but, in a modern England. These episodes were extremely well written, with first-rate humor and displayed superb knowledge of what is referred to as the "Canon" *(Arthur Conan Doyle's original Holmes adventures).*

In Ross K. Foad, the whiz kid architect behind "No Place Like Holmes", I had found an innovator, a trailblazer, someone who was at the cutting edge of a new genre in the progression of the media characterizing of literacy's most famous character, Sherlock Holmes.

For over thirty years I had collected photos and autographs of actors who have played Sherlock Holmes and Dr. Watson, on stage, radio, TV, and in film. Every one of these medians had it's own section in my collection, filled with innovators and brilliant performers.

Stage, had Charles H.E. Brookfield & Seymour Hicks as the first to ever play Holmes & Watson in "Under The Clock" (1893), and immortals such William Gillette and H.A. Saintsbury, each with over 1,300 performances.

Film, had Maurice Costello as the first credited Sherlock Holmes in "Held for Ransom" (1905), and greats such as John Barrymore, Eille Norwood, Arthur Wontner, Basil Rathbone, and Robert Downey Jr.

Radio, had Edward H. Smith in "The Sign of The Four" (1922) (WGY - Schenectedy, N.Y), (most 'experts' would erroneously tell you it was William Gillette or Clive Brook), it also had the genius of Orson Welles, and of such duos as, Basil Rathbone & Nigel Bruce, and Clive Merrison & Michael Williams.

Television; had it's first Holmes' actor in Louis Hector in "The Three Garridebs" (1937), and greats like Ronald Howard, Boris Karloff, Douglas Wilmer, Peter Cushing, Visiliy Livanov, Jeremy Brett and Benedict Cumberbatch.

But this was something new entirely; I contacted Ross K. Foad and Mike Archer to request autographs, and explained my collection to them. What happened next can be summed up best by the famous movie line, by Humphrey Bogart in the movie classic "Casablanca", "Louie, I think this is the start of a beautiful friendship."

Ross and Mike happily met the request, and they are now immortalized as a part of "The Holmes & Watson Collection". Ross even went a step further, when he discovered the collection was not being displayed anywhere, he created a virtual gallery at "No Place Like Holmes" to display what he renamed "The Howard Ostrom Collection" for all to enjoy. However, one dilemma still existed, "No Place Like Holmes" - do we place it in an Internet section, Youtube section, Social Media section, or Fandom section? I am not sure. What I do know, is that my collection needs a new unique section for "No Place like Holmes", its imitators and successors.

**Howard Ostrom**
**March 2013**
http://www.nplh.co.uk/the-howard-ostrom-holmes-and-watson-collection.html

## The Story Behind No Place Like Holmes - 2009
## The Fall And The Rise:

*"What do you mean you want to break up?"* I proclaimed aghast.

*"Breaking up is what ill matched married couples and arrogant boy bands who then cynically reunite for a re-union tour the next month do".* Though we were both boys, I was pretty sure none of the rest of the statement applied to us.

*"You're bringing me down man, I will get type cast working with you and we will never get anywhere just doing what we do"* replied my supposed best friend of the previous ten years.

Together *CHROSSTOPHER* were successful YouTube sketch comedians and a popular booking on the London comedy club circuit. We had won three Talentfreak.co.uk contests as well as the *"Clip Star Comedy Division Champions"* so all in all I had to disagree. Yet despite the accolades Chris felt it was my fault we were not progressing quicker, he believed my writing and decisions were holding him back.

If I can jump back a decade briefly, Christopher and I had met at secondary school in 1999. We had been working together as a published comic strip writer and artist team since 2001 before turning our hands to the exciting new world of YouTube and later on to the live comedy circuit. However, there was somewhat of a friendly rivalry underlying our partnership and guess what kids, it turns out there is no such thing as a friendly rivalry for very long.

Looking back what is quite funny is a lot of the humour came from the fact that none of our characters ever got on and bickered endlessly. Our sketches tended to have a high level of energy, were rife with word jokes, and generally had appeal to the young and old. Oh yes and often involved hats *(All things I believe I have gone on to replicate in "Ross K Reviews")*.

**Chrosstopher at the Comedy Pub London 2009.**

**Our sketches were generally bananas.**

However, this style we had developed was not truly Christopher's cup of tea. Christopher preferred the more obscure styles of humour that had begun emerging from the early-mid noughties. The type where drugs, sex, making people uncomfortable and talking about taboos for the sake of talking about taboos were the norm. This type of humour does not sit well with me and as a result I vetoed many of his ideas to incorporate this into our acts.

Undeniably we had dynamic performance chemistry with one another. Chris was hugely talented as a performer and video editor, but utilizing it in a practical or business sense did not always come easy to him. Hence why I took the lead with being the head scriptwriter, why I decided what to perform and why I managed our bookings and promotion, all of which continued to drive a wedge between us.

**Any claims I am egotistical are all highly inaccurate, anyway here I am playing God 2009.**

**We often tackled serious issues in the sketches..like co-co-pops addiction.**

The fact we were not at The Apollo, nor have our own TV show or action figure led to his disillusion with the team, sadly he did not see the success we did have but only the larger scale success we did not have.

To cut a long story short, much to my dismay that was the end of CHROSSTOPHER with our final performance being at the Comedy Store in London one rainy day in November. Chris left to perform stand up musical comedy as Rollo the Hippy who sang about mustard *(I am not making this up)* for a few months before promptly disappearing into the ether. I still believe had we carried on we could have gone very far but alas, it was not to be.

This is how I found myself needing a new idea to continue my YouTube ventures. I knew I could not give up what I had been doing the past few years for good because writing and acting was too much fun but I could not for the life of me think what to do. The second problem was Chris had been the one who had learnt to edit and frame shots, the little I knew came from watching him do it.

For some reason this did not deter me though. I began to look at the possibilities of what I could do on my own and looked over previous unmade sketches scripts I had written for some sort of inspiration, nothing stuck out as anything I simply had to create until I remembered an unused Sherlock Holmes related sketch.

It placed the Victorian Holmes and Watson warped into the present day and being generally baffled by modern day gadgetry, I had always wanted to film it but felt it was not something I wanted to just use as one off sketch as had the potential for so much more.

Victorians, mystery and strong duo partnerships are individually all attractive traits for a story to me so perhaps it is not surprising that the world of Sherlock Holmes has always appealed to me. There is something magical about Doyle's words. His words transport me to the cosy sitting rooms of 221B and the foggy bitter gas lamp lit streets of London, my imagination would run rampant reading the stories.

The tender fleeting moments of friendship between Holmes and Watson, the genius methods of deduction and revelation when Holmes unwound a crime, larger than life characters, a time when people were polite (*well not Holmes always...*) and wore hats! Stereotyping at its best/worst and oh not forgetting the language and dialogue, I re-read sentences seconds after going over them simply because they are so deliciously constructed.

The more I thought about it the more I wanted to do it; I had visions of grandeur for it with everything I love about episodic television show. Ongoing plot lines, story arcs, deep character development *(it is for these reasons I have always much preferred the median of television series over films, its harder for me to care about characters I see for 90 minutes then one I see on a frequent basis and learn to grow with)*.

All of these ideas effortlessly began to flow freely into my mind effectively writing themselves but still there remained an element of doubt; I had neither the real technical know how and how could I convince others to join me in this adventure?

The catalyst came in the form of my elder brother Patrick *(Moustache Wax Baron/Make Up Artist/ 2nd Place in the British Moustache Championship)* who at the time was working on Guy Ritchie's Sherlock Holmes film. He suggested I should make my own Sherlock Holmes series and I would be perfectly suited to doing so, I was astonished by this as had never openly said anything about NPLH to anyone and proceeded to tell him my vision for "No Place Like Holmes".

He loved the idea and convinced me it needed to be done…even if his motivation was purely he wanted to make moustaches for the show. However he was right, this did need to be done, I had no idea how it would be but by God I knew I would make this happen.

As quickly as *CHROSSTOPHER* had fallen, the rise of No Place Like Holmes had begun.

# 2010.
## The Road Holmes Is No Easy Path.

After writing the first episodes pilot the first problem was casting Watson. It was difficult to pitch in one sense. Most acting positions have a fixed or estimate of the duration of the project set out from the get go. But here I was trying to convince someone to potentially sign up to commit for something that I had no idea for the length of nor could make any real promise of how much it would boost ones profile to be part of this.

Regardless, there was still an awful lot of interest in the roles and I found myself with over 110 applications for the role of Watson. Awful being the operative word here. Not one single actor bore any resemblance to the Watson of Paget's pictures, not one single actor had the warmth or controlled quiet temperament that matched the good doctor Doyle's words depicted. It was somewhat disappointing to say the least.

However, at this time I had begun teaming up sporadically for one off sketches with an old primary school friend of mine Samuel Coe. While Samuel would be the first to admit, he was not an actor in any traditional sense nor had desire to go down the road on any larger scale. What he did have was a willingness and enthusiasm to my idea, a quiet nature to contrast my quicker paced erratic portrayal nicely, plus undeniably a good look that made many find him very watch-able.

He also was actually a lot better than many of the people I had auditioned so I decided he would be the most suitable I could muster, besides this was a pilot episode essentially who knew if this would really go anywhere.

I rounded up the team with an actor by the name of Jack Davies to play Sir Hugo Baskerville, Jamie Stevens a stage design student hungry for cinematography experience and my brother as a makeup artist. So after quick negotiations for everyone's availability the date was set and we were good to go....or so we thought.

Working for No Place Like Holmes does sometimes for reasons out of my control require a degree of improvisation and quick thinking, the first day was no exception to this. Jack Davies failed to turn up *(note that name casting directors!)* and was not contactable by phone; things were going horribly wrong before we had even had a chance to utter the first lines.

What happened next I think will always be the moment I love my brother for most, he there and then offered to step in and play the role of Sir Hugo Baskerville. With his then flowing locks and epic moustache *(did I mention he won 2nd place in the British Moustache and Beard Championships...I did...oh...)* he had the perfect looks for the villainous role.

**My Brother as Sir Hugo Baskerville.**

But what is even more remarkable is while he had a good degree of success as a professional child actor, it had been more than 10 years since he has stepped in front of a camera having gone down the route of behind the scenes work, so to voluntarily agree to this meant an awful lot to me.

An outstanding performance from my brother, some brilliantly filming works from Jamie Stevens *(including dropping down to his knees and crawling to imitate a hound)* and a lot of laughing later we were wrapped and done .

Despite the limitations of low-grade DV camera recording, basic editing skills and a great dollop of cheese on top, somehow the 2-part pilot still struck a chord with Holmesians and former fans of *CHROSSTOPHER* alike. The views slowly crept up and comments began cropping up expressing particular enjoyment to the humour and the acting behind it.

There was enough positive reception from viewers and cast alike to convince me I had done ok. I knew I would be able to take a shot at carrying on my vision and continued with the rest of the first series.

**Samuel Coe and myself in the pilot episode "Moving Forward".**


## A Dubious Adversary

I could not possibly pass through 2010's history without mentioning the episode "The Dubious Spiritualist" this is still one of my all time favourite episodes to date because everything about it just seems to work on so many levels, should I ever get the opportunity to produce a second volume of more scripts I would certainly compile that within it.

By this stage Holmes had a home, he had a new housekeeper in the shoe obsessed Miss Blake *(played by the wonderful Tamzin Dunstone)*. With these key points now established it was possible for Holmes to return to the good old basic set up of a client calling upon Holmes with a peculiar problem.

It has red herrings, a twisty yet easy to follow plot, plenty of graveyards, smatterings of Doyle quotes as well as Granada nods too. The episode also acts as the first time we are introduced to the series antagonist Madeline Chambers, a descendant of the niece of Professor Moriarty whose overall role and involvement within the story arc becomes more apparent as the series progressed.

Originally the role of Madeline was supposed to be "Matthew" but I just could not find a male actor I truly felt was suitable for the role, there had to be a vindictiveness about them, the ability to portray the coldest of hearts and to have an aggressive vicious streak yet still play it for laughs. Sadly nobody I auditioned for the role over 3 months struck me as right and so I decided to change tact by altering the role to a female to see who it would attract.

Enter Kelsey Williams; an experienced stage actress and then drama student at Kingston University looking for her first piece of screen work. She might have stood at just above 5 foot tall but she had a certain fire to her, I could see she would have the ruthless streak required *(on screen at least...in real life she is as sweet as sweet could be)*. Plus she had recently done a run as Beryl Stapleton in a stage production of "The Hound Of The Baskervilles" which helped sway me she would be right for the job.

**Emma Lillie Lees and Kelsey Williams as Elanor and Madeline Chambers**
**"The Dubious Spiritualist".**

What I also like about this episode is it gave me the chance to show Holmes use of passing judgement over someone's crimes, how he often ignores the law and makes the moral judgement himself as to who should get away with a crime or not. I cite "The Speckled Band" as being the best canon tale which illustrates this trait to us.

## Brother Where Art Thou?

Another key point in the history of NPLH for 2010 would undoubtedly be the acquisition of James Ian Gray as Mycroft Holmes. I was keen to do some adventures covering the "Great Hiatus Years" of Holmes within the series, after all in "The Empty House" Holmes seems to sum up to Watson his previous three years of absence within a passage or so and little more is mentioned on this again. I figured it would be fun to examine what he got up to as Sigerson the Norwegian explorer in further detail.

Watson obviously would not be able to be in the adventure itself so I decided this would be the best chance to add Mycroft into the mix, after all he was the one who knew Holmes was still alive after the fall.

However, knowing how lazy Mycroft Holmes is, having him trudge around so actively for such a long duration would not have made sense. His role would be a more sedative one of turning up to offer intelligence, advice and for some reason as it would turn out... satsumas.

11

I contemplated a Pinkerton agent being Holmes active assistant in the case before deciding to go down the speculative fan favourite route and implemented an old Holmes story and theory that had done its rounds in society's discussions.

Namely, the old chestnut Holmes met up again with Irene Adler during his Hiatus Years and they fathered a son together. While I did not adopt the second part of the idea, to me it had potential for working with in the series; it would also give me an opportunity to work with Karin Rydle once again who had appeared as Adler briefly in a flashback sequence in "The Dubious Spiritualist" episode.

But finding the right man for Mycroft was again by no means easy, I wanted someone very tall, large build and with a certain level of eccentricity. Plus they also just had to have a magical Mycroft essence to them.

I did end up with a good deal of quality applicants who were sadly outside the desired age range, many would not have fit in with the fact the canon main characters as a whole in NPLH are younger than they would have been in Doyle's Canon. But where I can keep within Canon I will do therefore I needed someone to fit in looking seven years older than me so was looking for actors in the late 20's and early 30's.

I did not have a lot of luck till I confided in a friend over my problem in finding the right one, I described who I was looking for and what they needed to look like and she promptly suggested her friend James Ian Gray .

James came from Grantham Lincolnshire but had moved to Ealing (*West London*) a few years prior to work for the BBC utilizing his numerous skills as a camera assistant, video editor, sound technician and data wrangler. He had recently turned freelance though following his contracts expiration.

While James was not an actor he did have experience on stage during college years and she thought NPLH might be something he would be up for. After she showed me his photos I immediately had one of my casting director epiphany moments and knew this was the man for the job. He was six foot four, large build and above all else, he shared the last name of my favourite Mycroft Holmes actor Charles Gray.

**James Ian Gray as Mycroft Holmes "Holmes In Time For Christmas".**

Bizarrely enough he agreed to the idea and as it turned out when it came to actually filming, he was both an absolute natural and one of the funniest people I have had the pleasure to work with. Watch any of the blooper reels for *"Holmes In Time For Christmas"* *"The Creature In The Rye"* or The Mary Morstan Mysteries *"Hell Hath No Fury"* and you will see just how difficult it is to get through without him making us laugh.

HITC was a great success when it came out in the December of 2010, and though it may have been little over a year since *CHROSSTOPHER* had ended, I was starting to feel that maybe just maybe that was not such a bad thing after all.

# 2011
## Parting Ways.

2010 had been good to me in many ways and 2011 was off to a great start with the second series filming kicking off in early January. The show had an ever-growing audience, I had upgraded the DV over to an HDV camera, my editing had come along way and now we were ready to continue the rise. Then disaster struck, Samuel wanted out.

He did not feel comfortable doing more and to his credit openly admitted there could be someone better than him out there. I was aware of his growing unease for large line learning and when measured against some of the professional actors NPLH had begun to attract admittedly his performance came across as slightly weak.

Looking back, I can see now I subconsciously had begun to write to include him less because of it. It was Miss Blake who joins Holmes into *The Dubious Spiritualist* investigation instead of Watson, *Holmes in Time For Christmas* focus's on a hiatus story with the Holmes Brothers and Adler with Watson only in the opening and closing of the tale.

I felt torn because he had started this journey with me and was one of the very few who had placed faith in me to start the project but it was obvious he was right and I knew it. The series had grown a great deal by then and he had no idea it would become the commitment it now was. There was no animosity in his parting and he gave his blessings to find a new Watson to take over from him. The announcement was made on YouTube to advertise his resignation much to the disappointment of many fans and the new search was under way.

## Watsons Hiatus Year

As a result of Samuel leaving the first episode of the second series *"The Two Fold Bond"* had to have a large rewrite to have Miss Blake take the assistant role Watson was supposed to be doing in the episode. I knew halting production to find a new Watson could take a very long time indeed but this time around I was not going to settle for "*it will do*" but "*only the best will do*".

This as is turned out, was a blessing in disguise, what should not have worked effectively did. The pairing of Miss Blake with Holmes was an odd couple made in heaven as it turned out and the audience reaction was positive. The screen chemistry between Tamzin Dunstone and me was obvious very early on and not since my time in *CHROSSTOPER* had I felt so at ease working with someone.

**Miss Blake doing an excellent job during her shift in a stake out "The Absent Phantom".**

14

When I work with Tamzin it is so easy to lose myself and immerse into the action. This is both due to her outstanding acting ability but also because in truth Holmes and Miss Blake are only minor extensions of our own personalities, there is not much acting required. Tamzin is literally that obsessed by shoes and actually has a room for shoes in her house which at the last count held 56 pairs *(figure likely far higher than this by now)*, she also has the ability to identify when someone has bought a new pair of shoes within seconds of seeing them. I do believe she could even write a monograph on the subject.

Often my writing of our scenarios take inspiration from what Tamzin and I do off screen such as in the recent series three finale *"Dialysis Murder"* there is a scene I erratically pace up and down the room recalling the case facts to date forcing Miss Blake's gaze to ping-pong back and forth until she screams at me to stop because it is giving her a headache.

This was inspired from when she had asked me about a certain event a few months prior, for some reason I was unable to remain seated to explain it and indeed proceeded to pace the room back and forth telling the tale until she had to ask me to stop and finish the story sitting down. Art in the blood does take the strangest forms.

Essentially, looking back if Samuel had not been cast in the first place, the role of Miss Blake may not have developed further to what it is today which would be a crying shame.

We followed on the *"Two Fold Bond"* with *"The Absent Phantom"*. Not a traditional episode by any sense but when the concept of your show spirals from the suspension of disbelief that demonic time freeze rituals exist, séances are not exactly a radical departure really.

This was the first episode I brought my father into an acting role as the episodes client *(though he did do a voice over for The Two-Fold Bond)* and it was brilliant fun working with him for the first time on an actual production of something. Temur Durrani also returned to play The Spiritualist a second time though this time there was nothing dubious about him as he was firmly on Holmes side!

**Enlisting the help of The Spiritualist was child's play. "The Absent Phantom".**

This is also the episode with the creation of Miss Blake's infamous "Auntie Pat", an off cut remark she makes when Holmes and Miss Blake are supposed to be waiting in silence as they stake out the clients house overnight. As regular viewers will know Auntie Pat has since gone to become a frequent topic of interest Miss Blake insists on telling Holmes and Watson about whether they want to know or not despite them having never the bloody woman.

Meanwhile the search for Watson was still on, though no one particularly exciting had come forward there were two e-mails of considerable interest among them.

One was from an actress called Victoria-Jane Appleton who 18 months later would turn up in the show herself as Miss Bliss the librarian in the episode *"Reign Will Fall"*. She had noticed the role floating around the web and took it upon herself to e-mail me a list of actors she had encouraged to apply for the role believing them to be suitable *(though she had worked previously with Mike Archer at the time he was not actually one she considered!)*.

The other one was a direct application from a Lexi Wolfe who asked if I would consider changing Watson to a woman! Strange but not overtly radical for it had been done a handful of times before in television films years before. I wanted a traditional Watson so that was a thanks but no thanks but told her I would keep her in mind for a future role as she was a talented actress and a keen Holmesian who had always yearned to have some Sherlock Holmes related production to her C.V.

Obviously as it turned out she would end up playing **MRS**. Watson *(to be)* a year later as I ended up casting her in the starring role of Miss Mary Morstan in the spin off show *The Mary Morstan Mysteries*.

### Reviewing The Situation

During the summer of 2011 I had a dream, in this dream there was a giant lobster in a train which wanted to borrow gardening gloves, because this has nothing to do with anything to do with NPLH I will tell you about the vision I had when I was awake instead.

At this point I had started to get into reading Sherlock Holmes pastiche stories quite heavily *(Holmes stories not by Doyle)*. I was always aware they existed as owned a few but it was not until I really looked into I realised just quite how many there were. There were literally hundreds available to find on eBay and Amazon, I began to wonder how anyone would know which one to start looking for and what ones were any good. Some had a few lines of reviews on them, but many did not. I did manage to find the odd blog that covered more recent releases but not many addressing the back catalogues.

That is when I was hit with the idea for *Ross K Reviews*. I had a couple of these pastiche books at this stage so I thought I would re-read them and make notes of observation and possible interest breaking it down in three main categories for pastiches *(Writing Style, Plot, Canon Usage and Accuracy)* and three main categories for non fiction Doyle Holmes books too *(Writing Style, Education Value and Entertainment Value)*. I would then sit down and record a review of me talking about the book then give them a grade out of Six Napoleons.

I did not really have any inkling of the impact this would end up having for No Place Like Holmes as a brand. I thought I would do them occasionally in the lull of any episode releases just so I could have at least a video once a month coming out which was a minimum requirement for getting into the coveted YouTube Partnership scheme.

The first one went out in August of 2011 and was on Nicholas Meyers "The West End Horror", within a matter of hours I was astonished to suddenly be getting a great deal of detailed comments expressing very positive attitudes and inquiring as to when I would be doing more.

I obliged and followed up with "Young Sherlock Holmes Death Cloud" *(3/6 Napoleons, OK...but silly plot and a dull Holmes)* plus "The Seven Per Cent Solution" *(4/6 Napoleons, If you can get over the alternative Canon universe idea it is a rather good read and is one of the forefathers of Holmes Pastiches).* These were well received and I began to get requests to cover certain books and soon found myself being sent droves of Holmes books from authors and publishers in America and England eager to see my thoughts on their books.

I soon acquired some sort of reputation of trust where some people seemed to value my opinions and many began purchasing books they liked from the sound of my reviews and coming back to thank me for persuading them to look into it. I have to say this is one of the greatest pleasures of NPLH,  when I hear someone has enjoyed something I have recommended it makes me feel perhaps what I say may have some degree of merit after all. What started as a gap filler I soon realized was so much more thus *"Ross K Reviews"* became incorporated as a permanent regular companion show under the NPLH brand.

To this day though, I have to confess I still do not quite understand why people seem to like them. But as far as most authors go, I can only figure it is something to with it is 10 minutes of someone literally talking non stop about their book, something they have invested hours of their life and soul into. Or maybe its because I wear costumes and make puns…I honestly don't know.

## The Arrival Of Archer.

While Watson's hiatus year seemed set to continue I returned to a retelling of another of Holmes own hiatus years with *"The Creature In The Rye"* which followed on from the events of *"Holmes In Time For Christmas"*.

The tale involved Sherlock being called out of hiding by his brother to engage in a hunt for a kidnapped minister's daughter taken by a mysterious beast and the beast master. The episode saw a further guest appearance from the excellent Mark Saint John Ridley as Colonel Sebastian Moran who in my mind is a criminally under-appreciated actor and to me the very definitive Sebastian Moran. In the episode he is joined by Tonga the Savage played by Simon Grewal who had also been a gypsy in "A Game Of Shadows". Funnily enough, the location used to film this episode (*Richmond Park*) was also the exact same place he had filmed in on "A Game Of Shadows".

**Colonel Sebastian Moran(Mark Saint John Ridley) and Tonga The Savage (Simon Grewal)**
**"Creature In The Rye".**

I enjoyed doing this episode a great deal but was beginning to despair over the struggle to find someone worthy to take the role of Watson and knew I could not keep up the show forever without one. I was still receiving many applications and running auditions but still no one felt right for me. However, just as Tamzin and I were preparing for the 2nd season finale *"Hats Off Mr. Holmes"* my prayers were finally answered.

Having trawled all the well-known acting sites repeatedly, I decided to try an advert on Mandy.com, something I use very rarely and not the best known of them. I figured that maybe just maybe someone of merit might come forward.

Shortly I got a bundle of response forwarded on to me but my heart began to sink as I read them. It is painfully obvious to a casting director when an actor is applying for the sake of applying without truly being interested in the project or has even read the job. My particular irritations are copying and pasting the exact details of a profile page as an application message, making no reference to the role/project and why they are suited or saying "I am exactly what you are looking for" when they do not match literally one of the requested physical traits.

Suffice to say there were plenty of these among them. Dispirited I selected the rest of them without opening and hovered the mouse pointer to delete, I was just about to click when my eyes scanned the names on each one last time when suddenly I paused…Michael Archer.

From the second the words left my lips I liked the sound of him. That was a strong British actor name for sure. I unclicked his email from the deletion firing line and opened it up.

Now I do not know much about the notion of love at first sight but one thing is for certain, Boswells at first sight surely do exist and here was mine starring at me in all his Jpeg glory.

He had a perfect Watson moustache, his physical traits matched, background in theatre, his nickname was "Period Mike" due to his extensive array of history-based productions, he was three years older than I was which matched the believed age difference between the detective and doctor. His message told me he wanted to express his "deepest interest" into the project and playing Doctor John Watson. Not just interest, DEEPEST INTEREST! And look, he actually knew the name of the character that he was applying for.

I knew this was the one for me there and then and promptly arranged for his audition piece rewriting an alternative version of the episode *Hats Off Mr Holmes* to include Watson for him to audition with and what can I say, my instincts proved right.

It was on October 31st 2011 that Mike Archer became cast officially into the prestige role of Doctor John Hamish Watson M.D and at long last, Watson had finally come home.

I shall now briefly pass you over to him so you can hear the thoughts from the mind of the man behind the moustache.

**I might be the master of observation but I never noticed Watson looked remotely different since I had last seen him.**

### MIKE ARCHER ON BEING WATSON
**"The doctor is in the house"**

Little did I know when I took on the role of Dr. John Watson, I was entering a world which was already well on it's way to becoming a hit with the Sherlock Holmes internet community. So there is a certain amount of pressure when one takes on a role that is as classic as Watson and even more so when you are filling the shoes of another. It was a little scary but at the same time the role presented me as an actor with a fantastic opportunity – to not try to replicate the previous incarnation, but to adapt the preconceived ideas, smash them to bits and bring to the table 'my' interpretation of Watson. Believe me when I say this is something which every actor aspires to.

19

I was keen to develop a relationship between Holmes and Watson that was different and presented an interesting dynamic for the series. There have been many interesting combinations of the duo and I wanted to find something that was slightly contemporary but still honoured the traditional view of Watson.

Aspects of the character such as the moustache and cane are part of the physical identity of the character and they had to be there but to me their relationship is the friendship that shouldn't be... but is. The closest of friends who pull pranks on each other to wind each other up or have the ability to speak their minds about each other when they get agitated. But these are two men who have the fondest of cares for each other.

For me Watson needs Holmes as much as Holmes needs Watson especially when they emerge into the modern world. It is their dealing with the crazy situations this world throws at them and their perception of the weird world we live in that makes for such interesting comedy. Watson is a modern man and that allows him settle into the new time frame easier than Holmes (that is not to say he's about to adopt but he has adapted) .

Key to unlocking this is the improvisation and it is through this I was able to develop Watson's relationship to Holmes. It is this improvisation that makes a 'No Place Like Holmes' set such a fun place to be. Some of the funniest moments and bloopers come from our messing around with the lines or the situations but it lends a strength to their relationship.

'No Place Like Holmes' has grown significantly since I stepped into the shoes – a definite highlight being included in Howard Ostrom's collection as the definitive Watson and Holmes of the internet is a testament to the strength of Ross Foad's vision for the series. Where the crazy modern world will take Watson will reveal itself only in time, but what ever it is – it's going to be a tremendous amount of fun when "the doctor is in the house".

**-Mike Archer**
**April 2013**

**Holmes tells Watson he could pretend to be a doctor to get into the surgery.**
**"Dialysis Murder" 2013.**

# 2012
## The Entities Expansion

Coming in from 2011 things were looking good. The early part of the year was spent on the filming of the spin off show *"The Mary Morstan Mysteries"*. Set between the years of 1889 with the intention to run to 1892 which would serve to allow deeper integration of Canon usage and allow for cross over back story elements into No Place Like Holmes. It also meant NPLH as a whole uniquely offered Victorian set stories alongside the modern day set stories.

It was also a chance for me to take a step back slightly and not be as heavily involved directly on screen as I had been in the main NPLH series which was a slight relief. Do not get me wrong I have no problems with taking centre stage, but you have to remember I was also the one responsible for arranging everything pre and post production for this shows existence, from writing it to casting it to sorting the schedules to directing on set and then editing the finished pieces. All positions I relish actually doing and would not relinquish any of them, but all this on top of the book reviews and actually making a living...well it did take its a toll on my already ebbed away sanity after a while.

Through MMM and the fact I had a Watson again meant I was able to slowly reign back *some* of the time I needed to spend line learning, doing MMM episodes instead of just NPLH episodes for the year gave me some extra time . Yes I had a large role in the pilot *"Wheres Wheres Watson"* and a support role in *"Hell Hath No Fury"* to ease the transition and effectively train Miss Morstan but it was still less than if I had been doing solely NPLH episodes with no Watson. And that was all vital time I needed to allow for what was coming next.

**Miss Mary Morstan (Lexi Wolfe) has words with the security guard at parliament played by her real life other half Jonathan Wolfe in the MMM Episode "Hell Hath No Fury" 2012.**

**Toby the dog makes an appearance in the MMM Episode
"Wheres Wheres Watson" played by my real life dog Bilbo.**

## GSHD

No Place Like Holmes was on a rise there was no debate about it, but what there was a debate about was The Great Sherlock Holmes Debate 2 *(Actually the same as the first one which took place in November 2011 but done on a grander scale as the first was solely a web chat)* .

The debate organized by MX Publishing would see a group of Holmes authorities, actors and authors come together including Charlotte Anne Walter *(Barefoot on Baker Street Author)*, Roger Johnson *(Holmes Society Of London)* and Nick Briggs *(Voice of Holmes in Big Finish audio adaptations)*. To compete in a debate over the BBC's Sherlock series VS Warner Bros Sherlock Holmes franchise. Participation included 10 lucky fans via web seminar technology to allow them to listen in to the debate live and watch the power point presentations.

I came to be involved after coming to the attention of Steve Emecz the Managing Director of MX who invited me to be part of the Warner Bros team and conduct some video interviews with some of the participants. This was a hugely flattering offer but ultimately I ended up passing this by in favour of offering to capture and edit a video of the debate itself. The video series proved to be a great success with thousands of Holmes fans worldwide viewing and enjoying them *(the videos are still available on the NPLH site if you want to watch them yourself)*.

It also brought me more into the Sherlock Holmes community's eye as a whole having previously been skating somewhat on the outskirts of really having any interaction or attention from the other groups and organizations. But what was even better was a result of the popularity of the live debates further ones were planned for the future and the rights to future debate video coverage was offered to No Place Like Holmes.

Securing these was a huge status boost for its profile and meant it was another unique video offering NPLH would have in its line up to go alongside the series and book reviews.

**Nicholas Briggs and "Big Finish" Audio Adaptations producer Martin Montague
at the Great Sherlock Holmes Debate Two.**

## Summer Of Sherlock

The Summer of 2012 was a great time for NPLH and The Sherlock Holmes World altogether.
The first ever "Sherlock Holmes Week" was run with Holmes organizations world wide
arranging events and competitions for fans. NPLH ran a voice actors role contest with the
chance for any Holmes fan to send in an audition to voice an off screen character in the next
NPLH and MMM.

"The Great Sherlock Holmes Debate 3" took place (*Best Sherlock Holmes Story*) and the third
series of NPLH kicked off with "*Red Rising*". The Sony HVR-1AE HDV camera I had been
using for the second series was retired in favour of a Z1 (*which at time of writing is due to be
retired shortly*) upping the shows visual appeal further. Green screen technology also began
being incorporated more frequently allowing for more interesting locations and situations to
be utilized.

The episode *Red Rising* is actually the one I always refer new comers to the series to watch
first as opposed to the pilot episode hence the inclusion of it in this volume scripts first.

Aside from having a higher production value all around. Within the first eight minutes alone
*(Part 1)* you have the concept of the show and its general feel all rolled into one. It
established and sums up what year the show is set in, how Holmes and Watson are in the post
millennium era, their living arrangements with Miss Blake, and offers a glimpse into just one
of the many problems being a Victorian in the present day brings.

This was also the episode where the knots really begin to tie up and it becomes apparent
certain events of the previous two series were not entirely random and it really kicks off the
start of showing the depth there actually is to the story arc.

Lastly, it is of note that this was the episode that Mike Archer and I truly felt the bond of Holmes and Watson. We had figured out our places in our interpretation of the relationship. I think the moment I felt it truly had clicked into place was during the filming of the scenes when Braderick Theobald limps away down the alleyway and Holmes and Watson watch him while having a conversation about why Watson is not allowed a catchphrase when Holmes has several. When it came to filming close ups and the camera follows Braderick down the alleyway, there was no actual need for us to continue our part of the script further for we were then off screen and out of microphone shot. Yet we carried it on regardless and then broke into a lengthy extended ad lib version of it simply because A) It was fun and B) We could do it.

**Miss Blake(Tamzin Dunstone) expresses her dissatisfaction with Holmes and Watson's clothing "Red Rising" 2012.**

## Scholarships, Scars and Signings.

There were two events that took place in 2012 as a result of my work with No Place Like Holmes that I cannot even begin to describe how much they meant to me on a personal scale, obviously it would be rather lame of me to end there though so I can but try and explain why.

First, I was inducted as an honorary member of the *Nashville Scholars of the Three Pipe Problem* on the recommendation of Professor Marino Alverez and that came as a huge surprise.

I have no formal education past 15 largely because being born with Asperger Syndrome *(form of Autism)* meant I struggled a great deal with education. Not so much the actual obtaining and retention of information if it interested me as this is where the A.S plays in my favour. However, in secondary school social skills are survival skills and having A.S meant I had very few and therefore an easy target.

Amongst many other traits it means I have always had great difficulty with small talk and chatter, I am admittedly single-minded, aloof, I use over formal speech both verbally and in written format , I am preoccupied with my own agenda at the expense of others, indifferent to anything that does not interest me and I am happy to go an entire day without speaking to anyone. My performance as Holmes and my presentation for reviews is often commented on as quirky, it is not that intentional nor put on, my odd ticks and equally mocked and adored hand movements are because of the A.S.

Anyhow guess what! Oddly, none of this made me the coolest kid in school.

The Aspie brain also works in a way it never ends its intensely deep thought process, we have no control over that. Relaxation is almost impossible because the brain is constantly racing, processing, indexing information, analysing or replaying conversations and events repeatedly.

Because of this often the last thing we want is to be constantly surrounded by people feeding new information to us and making demands for more, it is simply too overwhelming and "shut downs" do happen. For every hour spent around people Asperger sufferers often need two on their own to be able to rebuild themselves.

Finally combine that with the school I attended being bright, loud and frankly rather smelly, my heightened senses were a constant cause for pain.

Individually I have coping mechanisms to tackle some of these problems, I have been able to learn to adapt the best I can to mask it where necessary for a limited time but it does take a lot out of me. So when I had all of these challenges rolled into one environment day in day out for five years, I think you might be able to see why my educational experience was not one I would wish to repeat any time soon.

Yes I still emerged with 12 GCSES but I carried the mental and physical scars of secondary school to a college I was reluctant to go to from the offset. Subsequently I left in three weeks ignoring everyone's warnings I would spend the rest of my life in minimum wage employment as a result. I was determined to make my own way, on my own terms and I could not or would not follow the herd.

So as a college dropout condemned by many as stupid. To be acknowledged, formerly recognized, and initiated as a "Scholar" by a highly respectable Holmes Society in a country that is not even my own for services to Sherlockonia. Well this meant the absolute world to me and truly, it went some of the way to finally starting to fade the scars of my past.

Please do not think of this as some sort of sob story though, it is simply the facts of the matter and in truth though I have struggled for years to come to terms with myself and my disability, I would not give up my A.S for anything or anyone. It is every bit of who I am and imbued me with the abilities, drive and ideas that have allowed me push my dreams forward.

Another of the reasons I have chosen to share all of the above relates to the theory of discussion of Holmes having Autism/Asperger Syndrome. I would say go back, read the previous passages again, now tell me what you think. Personally, to me I think it is a conceivable theory and why I can relate to him so much. But as Asperger syndrome was not diagnosed in Sir Arthur Conan Doyles time I do not think he intentionally figured he would give Holmes any condition. Possibly he witnessed these traits in others *(Joseph Bell is the main basis of Holmes)* and incorporated them into Holmes as just that, personality traits.

**Being Presented my Scholarship at The Criterion Bar London in July 2012.**
**Courtesy of Nashville Scholars** www.nashvillescholars.net

The second monumental event of huge significance in 2012 would have of course been the YouTube partnership contract I was offered in November 2012 following a talent scout contacting me through the site. The partnership allowed me to have access to a greater support network, greater tools and functions for YouTube and a hefty spending account for purchasing music/sound effects and the commercial licenses for my videos. The contract also made the episodes, characters and concept for No Place Like Holmes legally copyright in law to myself.

Above all this, what truly made it so special though was the fact that 3 years prior as *CHROSSTOPHER* we had seen a partnership as a close to unobtainable Holy Grail of a goal. We would have done anything to get one, then if I consider the group was split up on the grounds I was holding it back…well, need I say more.

## Autograph Hunters Paradise.

I do not think I can truly end the section of 2012 without a passing mention to the incorporation of *The Howard Ostrom Holmes and Watson Collection*. Howard has already gone into the details of this in the lovely forward he wrote, but I will just emphasize this is an outstanding collection of Holmes and Watson actors autographed photos and I am hugely privileged to be allowed to have this included under the NPLH Banner. If you have not yet checked it out I recommend you do.

It really does have such a great assortment from the likes of William Gillette, Mel Blanc *(Voiced a Holmes/Watson Warner Bros cartoon short)*, Meredith Henderson *(The Adventures Of Shirley Holmes)* John Neville and Donald Houston *(Study In Terror)*, Downey and Law *(WB Franchise)*, and as my own dear Watson and Howard have already mentioned, Mike Archer and Ross K Foad *"No Place Like Holmes"*.

**A huge, huge privilege to be included.**

## NO PLACE LIKE HOLMES
## SERIES 3 EPISODE ONE
## RED RISING

ORIGINAL RUN 21ST JULY - 5TH AUGUST 2012 (6 PARTS).

### CAST

SHERLOCK HOLMES.................................................ROSS K. FOAD
DR JOHN H.WATSON...........................................MIKE ARCHER
MISS CHRISTINE BLAKE..............................TAMZIN DUNSTONE
MISS MADELINE CHAMBERS........................KELSEY WILLIAMS
BRADERICK THEOBALD.....................................BARNABY TWYMAN
RABBI HYMES COLESLAW...............................GENE FOAD
AUCTIONEER (VOICE)....................................MATTHEW J. ELLIOT

## SCENE 1
## INT: HOLMES/WATSON LIVING ROOM

Scene opens to WATSON quietly writing in his journal, he is seemingly under dressed from his normal outfits wearing only a plain white shirt and dark trousers. MISS BLAKE is dusting the corners of the room humming to herself gently minding her own business.

> **WATSON V/O**
> My name is Doctor John H Watson
> M.D, I was born in the 19th
> Century but I am writing this
> today in the 21st Century…but
> please do not turn away
> dismissing this as the witterings
> of a mad man or this writing to
> be a fictional science tale for
> neither of those would be the
> truth

> **MISS BLAKE**
> What's the H stand for?

Watson looks up a little surprised and pulls back the journal as Miss Blake now peers over his shoulder at the page curiously.

> **WATSON**
> It stands for Hamish Miss Blake

Miss Blake nods knowingly as if this means something to her.

> **MISS BLAKE**
> Ah right right Hamish…ok I get it
> now…right

She turns around walking back the corners of the room to start dusting again and starts up humming again as Watson continues to write.

> **WATSON V/O**
> My life is certainly more
> colourful than it was a shade
> over 2 years ago, or just over a
> century ago depending on how you
> look at it…

Miss Blake is peering over at the book once again nosily.

                    MISS BLAKE
            What's the M.D stand for?

Watson looks up slightly surprised by her presence being so
close and sudden interruption.

                    WATSON
            Medical Doctor…

She nods wisely as she repeats this to herself before turning
once again returning to her task. Watson is satisfied she is
no longer going to interrupt so continues.

                    WATSON V/O
            I would like to think having Mr.
            Sherlock Holmes as such a close
            companion all these years has led
            me to learn some of his logical
            way of thinking…but the very core
            of this logical thinking was
            shaken somewhat following our
            encounter with the dastardly
            demonic Sir Hugo Baskerville…

He looks up from writing and glances at Miss Blake who is
still dusting away in the corner. He rubs at his chin mulling
it over in his mind before returning to his trail of thought.

                    WATSON V/O
            I confess its easy to scoff at
            the idea anyone can be possessed
            in this manner, but given Sir
            Hugo Baskerville had perished
            hundreds of years prior and the
            incantation curse he cast upon us
            led to myself and Holmes being
            frozen in the very fabrics of
            time for over 100 years…well I
            dare say I can offer many other
            explanations.

Miss Blake finishes dusting and hovers over to Watson once
again cocking her head slightly to the side trying to get
glimpses at his writing again.

                    MISS BLAKE
            How do you get those lettery
            things after your name then?

Watson glances up and caps his pen before leaning back
slightly on his chair.

                    **WATSON**
          Well Miss Blake one would
          ordinarily get them from some
          lengthily period of study or
          training


                  **MISS BLAKE**
          Oh well that's a shame…I would
          have quite fancied having some
          but I'm no good at all that
          training or studying thing, is
          there no quicker way?

She picks up a television guide magazine from the sofa and
sits herself down bristling through the pages.

                  **MISS BLAKE**
          Just there are some really good
          things on TV tonight



Watson frowns baffled slightly by the question before smiling
to himself.

                    **WATSON**
          Well…no Miss Blake, I think it
          would take considerably longer
          than a single day and the only
          thing that would be more
          instantaneous would be if the
          Queen were to give you an O.B.E!



Miss Blake continues to flip through magazine transfixed and
nods.



                  **MISS BLAKE**
          Oh right ok I'll do that then

Watson goes to open his mouth to point out the many flaws in
this idea but is distracted by the door to the living room
opening and Holmes strides in with a bounce in his step and a
clap of his hands.


He like Watson is dressed only with his white shirt and black
trousers.

                              HOLMES
                    Good morning Watson…good morning
                    Miss Blake

Miss Blake glances up from her magazine and looks over to him
excited.

                            MISS BLAKE
                    Morning…guess what! The Queens
                    giving me an OBO

Holmes shakes his head unsure if he heard correctly.

                              HOLMES
                    Ok…it is only 9 A.M and I cannot
                    even begin to tell you on how
                    many levels I am already
                    confused…in addition Miss Blake I
                    was not aware you were remotely
                    musical, you normally violently
                    object to my violin playing


                              WATSON
                    She means an O.B.E

Holmes nods appearing satisfied until it dawns on him what
exactly has been said.

                              HOLMES
                    Oh An O.B.E…ah yes yes…that
                    makes…EVEN LESS SENSE?? MISS
                    BLAKE IS GETTING AN OBE?

 Watson pushes his book away and shakes head frowning.

                              WATSON
                    No rather she wants one


                              HOLMES
                    OH wants one, oh no no no Miss
                    Blake you don't want one of
                    those, far more trouble than they
                    are worth…why do you remember
                    Watson TWICE Queen Victoria tried
                    to palm those poisonous honour
                    titles upon me and…

Miss Blake glances between them as Watson tries to get Holmes
attention clearing his throat loudly and tilting head it in
the direction of Miss Blake.

                              HOLMES
              …Goodness the difficulty I had
              getting brother Mycroft to remove
              my name from that list


                            MISS BLAKE
              Sorry? Queen Victoria?


                              HOLMES
              Queen Victoria…did I say Queen
              Victoria…haha! I of course meant
              um…Queen…Elizabeth…the…

He glances at Watson willing him to give him a hint when he
suddenly remembers and snaps his fingers pointing to Miss
Blake.

                              HOLMES
              Second! Haha silly me…I always
              get them mixed don't I overworked
              you see, lack of sleep, brain
              freeze and OH look TEA, Watson
              why not pour us a cup and tell me
              if there is anything of interest
              in the local paper

Watson raises his eyebrows as Holmes by habit reaches to
adjust his cravat only to find its not there.

                              WATSON
              Well, there was a rather tragic
              story of a young man…Braderick
              Theobald whom following a
              deferred prison sentence was
              doing some community service and
              was said to be turning his life
              around having taken a painting
              and decorating course

Miss Blake gets up off the sofa and slips past them
exiting the living room.

                              WATSON [CONT]
               But as he was doing the stripping
               and repainting of a Rabbi leaders
               house the blow torch backfired
               causing severe burning to his
               hands and he fell off the ladder
               too…poor lad…and huh and can you
               believe this Holmes, the wife of
               the Rabbi simply remarked
               "Typical youth of today whose
               going to finish painting my house
               red now"…huh the nerve of some
               people eh Holmes!


Holmes eyes wander the room as he shrugs non-committally.

                              HOLMES
               Mmm…tragic that may be Watson
               altogether irrelevant in the hear
               and now…anything else…?


                              WATSON
               Well bag snatching is on the rise

Holmes leans over and whips the paper off the table out of
Watson's hands so he can get a better look.

                              HOLMES
               Snatching you say? Tut now really
               what IS it with people
               nowadays…honestly…it is such a
               common place crime anyhow, no
               imagination in it

Holmes throws it casually over his shoulder causing the papers
to come loose and fall all over the floor.

                              HOLMES
               Right well there's clearly
               nothing of interest there SO
               Watson if you have nothing on
               yourself perhaps you would care
               to join me for lunch today, I was
               rather hoping to  see if Goldinis
               is still open after all this time

Watson ponders this for a second then leans forward in his
chair nodding clearly liking the idea.

                              **WATSON**
          What a splendid idea Holmes…I
          would be delighted to, so it is
          nine o' clock now so let us
          synchronize pocket watches and
          meet for thirteen hundred hours…

They both extract pocket watches and wind them to adjust
accordingly.

                              **WATSON**
          I must say though Holmes… if we
          are to be going out, I must
          ask…have you seen my cravat? Or
          my waist coat? I would not wish
          to look a half-dressed Harry
          whilst dining

                              **HOLMES**
          Ah no funny I was going to pose
          the same question to you dear
          friend, I appear to have mislaid
          my own cravat, waist coat AND two
          hats

There is a throat clearing noise cutting through the air and
Miss Blake has reappeared at the living room door leaning on
the frame and clutching hold of a bundle of freshly pressed
clothes.

Holmes and Watson turn to face her and Holmes points
enthusiastically.

                              **HOLMES**
          Ahah! There you are Watson
          mystery solved…Miss Blake has
          them freshly washed and pressed
          for us

Miss Blake's face remains stony and unmoved.

                              **HOLMES**
          She also has an exasperated look
          upon her face…err now what I have
          done?

Miss Blake takes two steps forward and frowns holding the pile
of clothes higher up.

### MISS BLAKE

Well its just…ok look ,I am sorry
I have to say this but you know
how fashion conscious I am, well
it's really bothering me now but
in the two years I've known you
and been your housekeeper…I've
only ever known you to wear *these*
type of clothes

She gestures to the pile whilst pulling a face of disapproval.

### HOLMES

Sorry what do you mean "these
types of clothes"?

Miss Blake shrugs and puts clothes down onto the table.

### MISS BLAKE

All I seem to wash for you two
are…tweeds, waistcoats, braces
and stuffy shirts my Granddad
wouldn't be seen dead in…

### WATSON

But I like tweed…

Holmes nods and points to Watson.

### HOLMES

He likes tweed

### MISS BLAKE

At first I didn't say anything
because I thought well…maybe you
dressed like that because you
were going to a fancy dress party

Holmes and Watson exchange puzzled looks.

### HOLMES

For two years?

**MISS BLAKE**

Well…yeah I mean you could have
just been like really really
excited about it, like how I've
already chosen the shoes for my
wedding!


**WATSON**

Wait wedding? What…when…who are
you marrying?

Miss Blake waves hands flippantly.

**MISS BLAKE**

Oh details details…I don't know
about that yet but ok I mean…

She picks up a top hat and deerstalker hat from the pile and
holds them out in front of her.

**MISS BLAKE**

Mr Holmes…*A* who wears a top hat
when it's NOT a wedding and *B*
please explain to me
what…THIS…with the…flaps…is?

Holmes snatches the deerstalker from her hands and scowls
before placing it upon his head.

**HOLMES**

Ok *A* I do obviously and *B* it is a
deer stalker…I wear it when I am
stalking deer…which evidently
enough is never but never the
less only a FOOL would question
the deerstalker

Miss Blake rolls her eyes then points to clothes.

**MISS BLAKE**

FINE but come on guys where are
your jeans? Your chinos, your
Polos and God where are the
names! Hugo Boss?


**HOLMES**

What?

                    MISS BLAKE
Ralph Lauren!


                    WATSON
Who?



                    MISS BLAKE
I mean it's…

She pauses suddenly and takes a sharp intake of breath.

                    MISS BLAKE
OMIGOD…I've got it…ok don't panic
boys I've got it…

Holmes and Watson exchange worried expressions as Miss Blake
claps hands together excited.

                    MISS BLAKE
…WERE GOING ON A SHOPPING
TRIP!!!!

Holmes looks increasingly uncomfortable and begins to eye the
French windows while Watson sits up sharply as he turns his
attention to an excited Miss Blake who is already throwing a
scarf around her neck.


                    WATSON
Shopping trip? I err well that's
very kind of you Miss Blake…and I
would love nothing more
but…Holmes and I really do have a
very pressing case at the moment
do we not Holmes?



                    *SFX*
            *FRENCH WINDOW SLAMS*

Watson looks on startled in disbelief as Holmes is now outside
and creeping along back to the French window pane.

                    WATSON
…Holmes…HOLMES?

Miss Blake waves hands as she places on her sunglasses.

                          MISS BLAKE
              Oh that's fine don't worry about
              him…we know his sizes you can
              help choose, now come on hurry up
              OH God we are sooo lucky you know
              today is Thursday, so you know
              what means? Late Night Shopping!
              We can be hours

She grasps his arm and forces him to stand and she starts to
pull him towards the door. He struggles to break free and
reach out for his tweed waistcoat upon the table as he is
dragged out.

                           WATSON
              Wait…no…hold on just a
              minute…MISS Blake! Can I please
              just get my waistcoat on…?

She continues to drag him out the door as he barely manages to
pick it up and throw around his shoulders.

                          MISS BLAKE
              Nope no time, No more tweed for
              you come on

As he is dragged out the door he turns his head and shouts out
in anger towards the French windows.

                           WATSON
              OH…BLAST YOU HOLMES!!!

                                              FADE OUT TO
                                              TITLE
                                              CARD




                                              FADE IN


SCENE 2
EXT:MARKET SQUARE

Amongst a revel of busy crowded shoppers, buskers and
bellowing market men Watson and Miss Blake weave their way in
and out of crowds. Miss Blake has her arm linked into his as
he observes the hustle and bustle of the town slightly wary.
His discomfort is not evident to her and she continues to talk
to him at a mile a minute.

                              MISS BLAKE
                    So I was thinking right...while we
                    are getting you your new clothes
                    we could also get me a new pair
                    of shoes!


                              WATSON
                    More shoes? Miss Blake...what of
                    the pair Holmes gave you for
                    Christmas

Miss Blake looks shocked and shrieks.

                              MISS BLAKE
                    CHRISTMAS!!! That was MONTHS ago!
                    I've bought like...fifteen pairs
                    since then

Watson shakes his head in disbelief.

                              WATSON
                    Fifteen pairs? I must say I
                    cannot see how it can be
                    practical to own more than
                    say...three pairs...when would you
                    get the opportunity to use them?


                              MISS BLAKE
                    WHEN! Oh John where to
                    start...where to start well first
                    there's Monday shoes...Tuesday
                    shoes...Wednesday shoes...Thursday
                    shoes Friday shoes, Saturday
                    shoes...Sunday shoes... AM and PM of
                    course


Watson nods but is frowning clearly unsure.

                              WATSON
                    ...of course

Miss Blake spots a shoe shop and drags him to the window.

                              MISS BLAKE
                    See those...those are nice...OH what
                    about some Vans...Vans are nice


                                40

                    **WATSON**
        Vans?



                  **MISS BLAKE**
        Yeah you know Vans…?

Watson shakes his head none the wiser.

                    **WATSON**
        No…

Miss Blake rolls eyes and drags him away.

                  **MISS BLAKE**
        Fineeee we will keep looking…


Miss Blake continues her tirade counting on fingers.

                  **MISS BLAKE**
            Anyway then there's shoes for
            parties, shoes for the beach…
            shoes for the park…shoes for
            snowy days…shoes for rainy
            days…shoes for sunny days… shoes
            for shoe shopping…shoes for
            graduation ceremonies… lazy day
            shoes…shoes for your best friends
            wedding…shoes for your *worst*
            friends wedding


                    **WATSON**
            Wait shoes for your worst friends
            wedding are different from shoes
            for your best friends wedding?

Miss Blake looks gob smacked that he would not know this.

                  **MISS BLAKE**
            Well…yeaaaah…obviously! The pair
            you wear to your worst friends
            will be better than the pair you
            wear to your best friends, you do
            not want to show up your best
            friend…but you do want to show
            OFF to your worst friend



                    **WATSON**
        I see…

                              MISS BLAKE
                    Then there are Birthday shoes
                    ...new years day shoes...Christmas
                    Day shoes...Boxing Day shoes...oh I
                    nearly forgot Hanukkah shoes.




                              WATSON
                    Hanukkah Shoes...? Miss Blake you
                    are not Jewish

Miss Blake rolls eyes and shakes head.

                              MISS BLAKE
                    Nooo but people I know are like
                    my Auntie Pat and Uncle Leonard
                    and...OMIGOD have I told you about
                    my Auntie Pat? She would just DIE
                    if she met you




                              WATSON
                    Oh how very nice...well I would
                    very much like to meet her too... I
                    am sure she would be very amiable
                    company




                              MISS BLAKE
                    Oh...no...no...no you would NOT want to
                    meet her she rubs people up the
                    wrong way all the time

Watson rests tongue against cheek clearly puzzled by the
sudden change of attitude.

                              WATSON
                    How so?

Miss Blake flicks wrist in flippant manner and makes a shadow
puppet talking motion with one hand.

                              MISS BLAKE
                    Talks too much oh she NEVER shuts
                    up...its just blah de blah de
                    blah...honestly

Watson nods and diplomatically then glances to another shop
window frowning.

                              WATSON
          Mmm…why would you pay one hundred
          and twenty five pounds for…

He is interrupted by Miss Blake shrieking and waving hands in
air as she spots a sign in the window.

                           MISS BLAKE
          25% OFF SALE!!!!! SEE…now
          THIS…this is what we like…come on
          don't just stand there lets go in

She links arms with him and drags him into the shop.


                                                  FADE OUT




SCENE 3
INT: HOLMES/WATSON KITCHEN

The door creaks open and slowly a hunched over Holmes peers
his head around the corner of it looking around uncertain.

                         HOLMES  [WHISPER]
              …Watson…WATSON…?

Not hearing a reply, he steps forward slightly before pausing
and wearily calling out.

                              HOLMES
              Miss…Blake…?

With still no reply he visibly relaxes and straightens up.

                              HOLMES
          Oh What a shame…left to my own
          solitude and devices…how ever
          shall I cope ? Sit in the dark
          brooding moodily or…hello what is
          this?

He picks up a leaflet off the letter rack on the side of
kitchen and reads from it muttering to himself.

                              HOLMES
              Police auction...unclaimed
              exhibits...seized objects and old
              police paraphernalia
              and its today; well that seems a
              jovial jaunt, much better than a
              "Shopping Trip", I think I will
              go and I shall head off
              immediately if not sooner

Holmes picks up his top hat from the kitchen counter and
throws his cane into the air catching it as he turns to head
out.

                              HOLMES
              Poor old Watson I really will
              have to make it up to him one
              day...BUT not today for it is off
              to the auction house for me

He strides out slamming the door behind him.

                                                   FADE OUT




**SCENE 4**
**INT: SHOP DRESSING ROOM**

Watson is dressed in a tight white t-shirt and jeans and is
patting the back pockets frowning. Miss Blake claps her hands
together and smiles.

                           MISS BLAKE
              Ohh yes THIS is more you


                            WATSON
              Is it...? I mean...I am not sure, it
              is not very practical...where would
              a person place his handkerchiefs
              in such a garb?


Miss Blake sighs and folds arms shaking head.

                                                   CUT TO

Watson is now dressed in a hooded top with the hood pulled up
tightly over his head, his hands rest in the pockets and he
stands slightly slumped as if a moody teenager. Miss Blake
nods in approval.

                    MISS BLAKE
          Now WHAT do you think of that?


                    WATSON
          I have an uncontrollable urge to
          go loiter around street corners
          now


                    MISS BLAKE
          Oh good! We will get Mr Holmes
          one too!

                                        CUT TO


Watson is now dressed in a leather jacket with aviator style
sunglasses.

                    MISS BLAKE
          Ohh YES…definitely


                    WATSON
          Definitely not! I cannot even see
          the mirror it's so dark…in fact I
          cannot see anything at all…

He reaches out blindly waving his hands unsteadily as Miss
Blake crosses her arms and rolls eyes.

                                        CUT TO


Watson is now dressed in a smart grey suit with a black trilby
hat. He looks down at it patting it seemingly satisfied.

                    WATSON
          Not bad…not bad at all…but Miss
          Blake…does it come in tweed?

Miss Blake throws hands into air and storms out of store in a
huff.

                                        FADE OUT

SCENE 5
INT: AUCTIONEERS HALL

Holmes stands amidst a crowd of bidders listening intently.
Next to him stands a black clad Rabbi in his late 50's also
listening and observing the crowd.

                    AUCTIONEER V/O
               Lot 221a, a shoplifter's packet
               of "Sherbet Lemon" left behind in
               custody…half of its contents
               remaining…the packaging promises
               a zing tastic time…do I have 10p?
               10 p? Come on 10p starting bid
               for a zing tastic time…yes sir
               you…15 p…now 15p

The Rabbi suddenly leans closer to Holmes and whispers.

                    RABBI COLESLAW
               What do you think my friend? I
               could go halves with you and we
               can share the zing tastic time?
               On the other hand, perhaps we
               sell on to another for a higher
               price than we paid…everyone is a
               winner!

Holmes looks very unsure of this and rubs chin.

                    HOLMES
               Well…I

                    AUCTIONEER V/O
               20p now standing at 20p…22 pence
               there…22 pence now standing at 22
               pence

The Rabbi throws hand in air in despair.

                    RABBI COLESLAW
               Oych forget about it…at that
               price…it's too much… my ugly wife
               she wants a dress…it's too much I
               say…too much
               true story

46

Holmes shakes his head baffled.

### HOLMES

Sorry?

### RABBI COLESLAW

That my wife is ugly? Oych so am
I no I kid...I could not do without
her...we have been married for 35
years...why? Because Government
offered lower tax breaks to
married couple so I thought why
not

### HOLMES

Quite so

### RABBI COLESLAW

Are you a buyer or a seller sir?

### HOLMES

Buyer potentially, I am somewhat
fascinated by the study of the
criminal mind so naturally there
may be some items on offer the
Police wish to do away with that
would be valuable to my line of
work...yourself? Buyer?

### RABBI COLESLAW

No seller...I make money not give
it away oych though I would
happily give away my ugly wife...no
I kid oych I have some auction
lots on after this one

### HOLMES

I see

### RABBI COLESLAW

Though I would be interested if
anyone was selling some
Strawberry Scarlett paint,it is
hard to get hold of…not a popular
choice…I need some more for I am
needing to finish painting my
house…I had a boy for free…
community service free…God sent
him…did I mention he was free?


### HOLMES

That cropped up yes…


### RABBI COLESLAW

Alas he burnt his hand with the
blowtorch and fell off the
ladder, my wife…she says "Hymes"
Hymes…that's me…"you hire someone
to finish this" but you know how
much they charge? So I said hey
forget about it I will do it
myself tchhh


### AUCTIONEER V/O

Lot 221b… Lot 221 b…for you
collectamaniacs and wannabe
criminologists…one finger print
case file from Scotland yard
dated for the South West of
London…2007-2009…every no good
scallywag who had his collar felt
in the area had his prints
recorded in this veryyyyy book.
But moving with the times all
have been transferred to
electronic files and this is now
surplus to requirement…a
fascinating piece of local
history…do I have five pounds?
Five pounds?

Holmes has taken considerable interest and wave's hand.

### HOLMES

Ten pounds!

**AUCTIONEER**

Ten Pounds I have TEN pounds! Do
we have more than TEN pounds?


**RABBI COLESLAW**

Fifteen pounds!

Holmes turns to look at the Rabbi and mutters.


**HOLMES**

I thought you were not buying


**RABBI COLESLAW**

I'm not, I just like seeing other
people spend money...less it is my
wife from my own wallet oych


Holmes shakes head scowling before turning back and waving
hand again.

**HOLMES**

Twenty pounds!!!


**AUCTIONEER**

SOLD to the man in the top
hat...Carstairs pass him the book!


**RABBI COLESLAW**

Why did you buy that? It is of no
value...a finger painting book no
more no less

Holmes raises eyebrows and is about to open his mouth only to
be cut off.


**RABBI COLESLAW**

Och...I kid I kid...I like you Sir,
we must come round to yours for
dinner...this is my card.

He hands Holmes a card, which he views with some suspicious frowning as he reads it.

                              HOLMES
                    "Rabbi Coleslaw - Pawn Broker
                    and…Circumcision Surgeon…"

                              RABBI COLESLAW
                    The card doubles as a coupon; we
                    are having a cut-price sale…a
                    snip of the regular price

                              HOLMES
                    I…well Rabbi Coleslaw

                              RABBI COLESLAW
                    Oh please, please we are
                    friends…call me Rabbi Coleslaw

                              HOLMES
                    I…yes well err I am sure we will
                    work something out…or not…good
                    day sir!

Holmes walks past him quickly as he waves frantically.

                              RABBI COLESLAW
                    Good day to you too sir, I very
                    much look forward to coming round
                    and eating your food for
                    free…yes?! It shall be zingtastic

                              AUCTIONEER V/O
                    SOLD to the chap with the
                    glasses…waving away frantically
                    to get his bid in…FIFTY pounds

Rabbi Coleslaw looks around in horror and holds hand to mouth gasping as he realises what he has done.

                              RABBI COLESLAW
                    Fif…Fif…Fifty Pounds…no no
                    no…och…what will my wife say…my
                    ugly wife…OCYCH

**SCENE 6**
**EXT:RIVER SIDE**

Open to Watson and Miss Blake strolling along the riverside.
Miss Blake has numerous shopping bags clutched in her hands
filled to the brim with clothes.

> **MISS BLAKE**
> What a morning! We should so do
> this more often BUT next time Mr.
> Holmes HAS to come

> **WATSON**
> Oh he will come don't you worry
> he *will* come…

> **MISS BLAKE**
> AND isn't your new cashmere
> sweater to DIE FOR!!!

> **WATSON**
> Well it is rather nice Miss Blake
> yes, I will grant you that…but I
> would rather not perish over an
> item of clothing

Miss Blake does not listen and looks out into the River at the
stalls and cafés.

> **MISS BLAKE**
> Right! I figure we stop for a bit
> of lunch, I know the NICEST café
> along here and then we can resume
> the shopping spree

She takes his arm into his as they continue to walk along the
path. A boat race is taking place upon the river and Watson
turns to watch with interest.

> **MISS BLAKE**
> So anyway, what drink do you
> think you will get with your
> lunch?

Watson slightly distracted shakes head and casts his attention
back to her.


                    WATSON
          Mmm? Drink…err…oh…a coffee

Miss Blake scoffs and waves hand laughing.



                    MISS BLAKE
          OH John you cant JUST have a
          coffee…



                    WATSON
          I can't…why ever not? Do they not
          serve them?



                    MISS BLAKE
          Well yeaaaah obviously but who
          has just "a coffee" these days…no
          what you would like is the *Frap-
          A-Dap-A-Mocha-Choco-Latte-Soya-
          Frotha-Chino*



                    WATSON
          Very well Miss Blake I shall try
          the Frap-A-Dap…err



                    MISS BLAKE
          A-Mocha-Choco-Latte-Soya-Frotha-
          Chino



                    WATSON
          Uh that beverage you just spoke
          of…

He pauses as his attention suddenly moves from her to the
river with considerable excitement.

                    WATSON
          I say over there…blessed be

                    **MISS BLAKE**
What are we looking at? Have you
seen a celebrity?!


                    **WATSON**
That boat! Over there…

Watson points to an old-fashioned looking trawler boat bobbing
up tucked near the pier. He walks closer to the edge to get a
better look.


                    **MISS BLAKE**
Oh…what about it?


                    **WATSON**
Well…it looks remarkably like The
Auroura…


                    **MISS BLAKE**
The Aww what what?


                    **WATSON**
The Auroura…I am sorry Miss Blake
of course you are not familiar
with this, The Auroura was a boat
Holmes and I pursued down the
River Thames err…many years ago
now…it was a case I entitled "The
Sign Of Four"


                    **MISS BLAKE**
The sign of four what?


                    **WATSON**
That boat…why I would swear it
was one and the same but it seems
impossible…it was so long ago…oh
if only I could show Holmes this
would certainly pique his
interest

Miss Blake folds arms bored now.

                              MISS BLAKE
                    So why not just take a photo?

Watson turns and laughs shaking head gently as he gestures to
his body.

                              WATSON
                    Miss Blake does it I look like I
                    am carting around photographic
                    equipment with me?


                              MISS BLAKE
                    Eh? No…use the phone I gave you
                    for your birthday

Watson appears puzzled but then light dawns in his eyes and he
extracts the phone from his pocket.

                              WATSON
                    The phone? OH YES…of course the
                    mobile telephone… it is a camera
                    too that is right you showed me I
                    remember now

Miss Blake rolls eyes unsure how anyone could forget this.


                              WATSON
                    So let us see…it was "Menu"
                    umm…"Call" …no that is not
                    right…ah…"Extras"…"Camera"…"Shoot
                    "

As he continues to fumble with the buttons behind Miss Blake
creeps a boy dressed in a black hoody. He picks up the
shopping bags by her feet and then tugs fiercely at the strap
of her handbag.

Miss Blake turns beginning a tug of war for the bag.


                              MISS BLAKE
                    Huh? GET OFF HEY NO DON'T YOU
                    DARE THOSE ARE DESIGNER…

Watson sees the commotions and rushes forward to them.

                              WATSON
                    HEY…UNHAND HER THIS INSTANCE YOU
                    ROUGE…

The boy appears panicked, with one last mighty tug he manages to take the handbag and darts off.

                          MISS BLAKE
          HEY!!!


                          WATSON
               COME BACK HERE YOU COWARD...

Watson chases after him full pelt but suddenly his leg appears to give out and he stumbles over.

                          MISS BLAKE
          JOHN NO!


                          WATSON
               DAMN YOU Jezali bullet

He dusts himself off and limps back to her.

                          MISS BLAKE
          John...are you all right?


                          WATSON
               It is just an old war wound don't
               worry about me, though are you
               all right?


                          MISS BLAKE
               He has my handbag MY LIFE is in
               that handbag! he's stolen my
               life! I have nothing left to live
               for

Watson places his hands either side of her arms to calm her.

                          WATSON
               CALM Yourself Miss Blake calm
               yourself...you are in shock...it is
               all right and don't talk daft you
               have ample to live for


                          MISS BLAKE
               We need to get after him we could
               catch up with him still...

                          WATSON
              He would be far gone by now Miss
              Blake it would be a waste of
              time…


                          MISS BLAKE
              Then we have to go the Police


                          WATSON
              And we will, but later…first I
              want to check you over
              properly…your safety here is my
              priority and then there's
              something else we need to do
              first


                          MISS BLAKE
              But what?

Watson smiles slightly deviously.

                          WATSON
              OH Miss Blake…I would have
              thought that was much was
              obvious…


                                              FADE OUT


**SCENE 7**
**INT: HOLMES/WATSON LIVING ROOM**

Open to Miss Blake curled up on the sofa looking very sorry
for her self. Holmes stands facing a painting on the wall with
his back to Watson who is watching him solemnly.


                          HOLMES
              So…let me get this straight

He steps forward and adjusts the painting slightly.

                    **HOLMES**
          There! I normally care very
          little for the state of the
          household…but this was just too
          crooked for words…

He spins on his heels and points to Miss Blake.

                    **HOLMES**
          Miss Blake! Watson! Back to the
          matter of the stolen handbag

                    **WATSON**
          I tried to run after him Holmes
          and I almost had him, why of all
          the times my Jezali bullet wound
          plays up now I will never know

                    **HOLMES**
          I am sure you did the very best
          your abilities allow you to do
          Watson, the important part is
          Miss Blake is safe and THAT my
          friend is a credit to you.

Watson nods pleased by Holmes praise and smiles slightly
despite his obvious sadness.

                    **WATSON**
          Thank you Holmes…but I wish I
          could have done more

                    **HOLMES**
          Your assistance may very well be
          required later on my dear friend
          but now it rests upon me, so you
          say you have not yet gone to the
          Police?

                    **WATSON**
          No Holmes ordinarily I would…but
          this is different

                    **HOLMES**
          Ordinarily I would not take on a
          common crime…but as you say this
          is different

He turns and motions to Miss Blake on the sofa.

                    **HOLMES**
          Now Miss Blake you got the better
          look at rascal…was he tall?
          Short?


                    **MISS BLAKE**
          Yes…


                    **HOLMES**
          Fat? Thin?


                    **MISS BLAKE**
          Yes…


                    **HOLMES**
          White? Black?


                    **MISS BLAKE**
          Yes…

Holmes head drops slightly as he rubs his eyes and sighs.

                    **HOLMES**
          …Miss Blake…you cannot answer yes
          to multiple-choice questions like
          that


                    **MISS BLAKE**
          Yes…no…ohhhhh I don't know I'm
          confused… I just want my
          handbag…OH he also took the
          clothes shopping Mr. Holmes and I
          had the nicest cashmere sweater
          for you too

                    HOLMES
          Well every cloud has a silver
          lining clearly.

Watson frowns at him shaking his head.

                    WATSON
          Holmes!


                    HOLMES
          BUT I digress…there is one key
          element that might prove our
          saving grace…he snatched at your
          scarf you mentioned…


                    MISS BLAKE
          Yes…his horrible nasty scarred
          grubby hands


                    HOLMES
          So he was not wearing gloves
          excellent…Miss Blake if I could
          have your scarf please

Miss Blake unravels her scarf and throws it to him.

                    WATSON
          Funny time to take an interest in
          fashion Holmes…

Holmes scowls at him as he catches it in one hand.


                    HOLMES
          Now it just so happens I have
          come into possession of a local
          goldmine of information. A
          compilation tomb of fingerprints
          for every caught criminal in the
          local area from the past few
          years, IF our snatcher has
          previous and is local…then there
          is a chance I will be able to
          identify him from the finger
          prints upon the scarf

                              **WATSON**
                    Brilliant Holmes! You really are
                    a genius

Holmes frowns and shakes his head.

                              **HOLMES**
                    Watson you have a horrible habit
                    of stating the overtly
                    obvious...but thank you

Holmes exits the room.


Watson goes and joins Miss Blake on the sofa; she is still
curled up on sofa looking heartbroken.

                              **WATSON**
                    Try and not worry Miss Blake if
                    anyone can get it back...Holmes can



                            **MISS BLAKE**
                    I don't think anything is going
                    to take my mind off this



                              **WATSON**
                    Don't think like that Miss Blake...
                    I know why not tell me what the
                    latest is with your soap
                    serial...television...thing

He gestures to her TV magazine lying on the sofa.
Instantly Miss Blake sits upright and becomes bright and
cheerful.

                            **MISS BLAKE**
                    Right well oh Gawd well
                    basically, you know Vicky? Well
                    her half sister Nicky she is
                    dating Ricky...ok but here is where
                    it gets tricky
                    because she's also dating Mickey
                    whose just pulled a sicky to go
                    on a stag do with his mate
                    Dicky......And THEEEEN Aunty Mo's
                    cousins hairdressers dog turned
                    up who we all thought was
                    dead...but it turned out right that
                    Phil cheated on his Doctors
                    exam........
                    AND I mean...like how clever is
                    that! I NEVEEEER Saw it coming

Watson blinks a few times saying nothing trying to process the story.

                         **WATSON**
              …Sounds very…interesting


                        **MISS BLAKE**
              Oh it is …you HAVE to watch it


                         **WATSON**
              …yes…I might just do that…

He politely smiles then stands up and walks out of room looking thoroughly confused.

                         **WATSON**
              …made about as much sense as
              Holmes's origins of the Piccolo
              story…

                                              FADE OUT


**SCENE 8**
**INT: HOLMES/WATSON FRONT ROOM**

Holmes is sat on the sofa deep in thought examining a cotton bud within a clear evidence bag that is tipped with red. Watson enters and walks towards Holmes slightly wary of disturbing him.

                         **WATSON**
              Holmes…I am sorry to interrupt
              but…


                         **HOLMES**
              I wish I could say you were
              interrupting but frankly Watson
              your not, I am getting
              NOWHERE…ugh sorry Watson go ahead
              with what you wished to say?

He throws the bag to one side and looks to Watson as he joins him on the sofa.

                    **WATSON**
          Well I was thinking…in the event
          we do not recover the handbag…

Holmes glares at him causing Watson to hold his hands up
defensively.

                    **WATSON**
          Not saying that we will not…but
          well wouldn't it be nice if we
          were to have a bit of a whip
          round? Get Miss Blake something
          nice after her ordeal…


                    **HOLMES**
          A whip round mmm what *all* two of
          us?


                    **WATSON**
          Well…yes


                    **HOLMES**
          A capital idea dear fellow…

Holmes takes Watson's hat that he was holding, turns it upside
down and after rummaging in his coat pocket places something
inside before handing it back.

                    **HOLMES**
          There you go…

Watson picks up the small card that is inside the hat.

                    **WATSON**
          Holmes, there is a coupon for a
          half price circumcision in here


                    **HOLMES**
          And I'm giving it to you! You can
          choose to pass it on directly or
          feel free to redeem yourself and
          donate the half price saving you
          make


                    **WATSON**
          Holmes…

                              **HOLMES**
          Not socially appropriate?



                              **WATSON**
          Not socially appropriate

Holmes rolls eyes and snatches hat back rummaging once more in
his coat before placing money inside hat.

                              **HOLMES**
              Fine…money it is…huh she is only
              going to spend it on shoes you do
              know that



                              **WATSON**
              Yes thank you Holmes……how you are
              getting on anyway?



                              **HOLMES**
              As I previously stated, I am
              not…there are three sets of
              clearly identified finger prints
              upon this scarf…Miss Blake's mine
              and your own

Watson nods to show he has understood as Holmes picks up the
bag once again looking at it closely.

                              **HOLMES**
              Then there is a fourth set of
              markings but I do not believe
              them to be fingerprints for they
              are too blurred and have no
              ringlet patters upon them…my
              identity book will prove to be of
              no use



                              **WATSON**
              But he grabbed it Holmes…I saw
              him…with his bare hands he
              grabbed it

                         HOLMES
          Was Miss Blake injured in the
          scuffle at all? Anything that
          would have resulted in minor
          breakage to the skin, a nick or a
          cut perhaps?


                         WATSON
          No she was not

Holmes pulls out the cotton bud and holds it to the light.


                         HOLMES
          Just upon the scarf there was
          some red flakes…an extract of
          which you can see here on this
          bud…oh well the old taste test I
          suppose…

He licks the nib then spits.

                         HOLMES
          Not blood…red paint…ahah in fact
          studying it in closer…Scarlett!


                         WATSON
          Holmes?

Holmes leaps to his feat excited.

                         HOLMES
          That's it Watson! I have a theory
          but some further verification is
          required to assure me I am indeed
          on the correct path. If my theory
          is correct…which lets face it is
          likely is… I need you to meet me
          in approximately one-hour's time
          in the alleyways behind the
          Priory primary school…oh yes and
          bring your service revolver.


                         WATSON
          Why?

                              HOLMES
                    Oh and I need this back…

He reaches into the hat and plucks out the coupon.

                              WATSON
                    Wait but Holmes your not Jewish?

Holmes Speeds out clutching it shouting as he goes.




                              HOLMES
                    ITS FOR THE ADDRESS WATSON…THE
                    ADDRESS…




                              WATSON
                    …Holmes??? What…but…your not
                    Jewish…HOLMES????

He hurries out after him.


                                                    FADE OUT


**SCENE 9**
**INT: TEMPLE**

Rabbi Coleslaw is counting out coins in one palm with a teddy
bear piggy bank tucked under his arm.

                        RABBI COLESLAW
                    One for Teddy…two for
                    teddy…another one for Teddy…oh
                    good one here for you Teddy

Approaching from the right hand side comes Holmes dressed in
an old thick grey sweater dungarees, a beanie hat and wearing
a thick moustache. He speaks with a Liverpool accent.

                              HOLMES
                    'Ello…Rabbi Coleslaw?

Rabbi Coleslaw jumps back slightly surprised and then becomes
suspicious.


                                65

#### RABBI COLESLAW
What is this? I hope your not
going to try and sell me some
expensive religious cult…if you
are you can forget about it I
already have a religion…but if
its free ehh I'll consider
listening


#### HOLMES
Nuthin of the sort chuck nothing
of the sort blimey stone the
crows perish the thought, I am
from "The Cheeky Chappy
Charity"…we heard about your
ordeal over your house and that
community service lad becoming a
cropper before he finished
painting your o'use


#### RABBI COLESLAW
My house…it is half red…this is
no good…tcch tchh


#### HOLMES
Exactly! That is what I said to
Reg I said "Reg you know that
Rabbi Coleslaw? Well his house is
only half-red". Moreover, as an
outstanding pillar of the old
community I am delighted to say
you have been nominated to have
the rest of the work undertaken
free of charge by our charity…

Rabbi Coleslaw eyes lighten up and he rubs his chin clearly
now swayed.

#### RABBI COLESLAW
Free? Well this is good news…when
can you start?

                    HOLMES
          Soon as we know exactly what
          colour red you were using…so we
          can source it right. So whatcha
          want Ruby Red, Raspberry Rouge or
          maybe Shade of Sheppard's
          Warning…?


                    RABBI COLESLAW
          No no it was it was Scarlett
          Strawberry…Strawberry
          Scarlett…here here I still have
          the colour chart from the DIY
          store

He takes out of a leaflet from his trouser pocket and flips to
the red section pointing to the red shade.
Holmes pulls it closer to himself to get a better look and
smiles to himself muttering in his normal voice.

                    HOLMES
          …perfect match

                                        FADE OUT


SCENE 10
EXT: ALLEY WAY

A young looking strawberry blonde haired scruffy male in his
early 20's is leaning against a wall with headphones on
nodding head gently to the beat of his music.

                    WATSON V/O
          You know who it is? What…how…?


                    HOLMES V/O
          All shall be explained in the
          fullness of time Watson all you
          need to know for now is our
          thief's name is Braderick
          Theobald of Black Peters Street
          which this ally is the back of…


                    WATSON V/O
          Well I never…our reformed well
          unreformed youth from the
          newspaper article this morning

                    67

                              HOLMES V/O
                    I hope you do not mind breaking
                    the law…for I may require you to
                    do some rough housing


                              WATSON V/O
                    As it concerns Miss Blake when
                    you like…where you like…


                              HOLMES V/O
                    Excellent…then it is going to be
                    right here…right now…there is our
                    target

Slowly from around the corner a hunched figure of an old woman
dressed in a white sweater, grey skirt and purple scarf comes
hobbling near to the male. She is seen to be clutching a
bright red handbag.


                              OLD LADY
                    Oh dearie me what a queue that
                    was at the post office…still got
                    my *pension now*…

She pats handbag for emphasis and continues to ramble loudly
as she dodders past the male who has taken off his headphones
and watching her with interest.

                              OLD LADY
                    But what a queue at the bank too!
                    Still got my withdrawal… …now I
                    can get my grand daughter a
                    lovely lovely birthday present…

Braderick has heard more than enough and greedily rubs his
hands before creeping up behind her and snatching at the bag
trying to prise it off her.


                              OLD LADY
                    AGHHH HELP HELP I'M BEING MUGGED


                              BRADERICK
                    Give me that! You are only making
                    it worse

He continues to tug causing her to fall to the floor.


                                 68

**HOLMES**

HELP!!!! Oh dear


**BRADERICK**

Shut up...stop screaming

Braderick looks around panicked hoping no one will hear her.

**OLD LADY**

I think I am having a heart
attack ohhh nooo...SOMEONE CALL A
DOCTOR

Braderick stands uncertain whether to help her or run before
turning to run but immediately is clobbered in the mid section
by Watson with a club.


**WATSON**

The Doctor is in the house!

Braderick lays by the wall winded while Watson crosses over
and pulls up Holmes whose disguise wig has slipped slightly.


**WATSON**

Miss Blake taught me to say that,
she said I should have a
catchphrase


**HOLMES**

Yes quite...well we will see about
that

Braderick has now risen to his feet and rushes to attack
Watson from behind.


**HOLMES**

Watson! look out...

Watson flings his arm backwards causing another blow to
Braderick's stomach before spinning around and grabbing him
from behind in a choke hold.

                    **HOLMES**
          Watson I am impressed... ordinarily
          its you who compliments me, but I
          must say your fighting skills are
          in top form today

Watson goes to open his mouth.

                    **HOLMES**
          Don't ruin it by saying...that
          catchphrase again...now as for YOU
          Mr. Braderick Theobald


                    **BRADERICK**
          Who on earth are you Super Gran?
          Whatcha want? Tell this guy to
          get off me

Holmes takes off the granny glasses.

                    **HOLMES**
          NO my name is Sherlock Holmes it
          is my business to know what other
          people don't know...and what I do
          know is this, you stole a handbag
          earlier today from my housekeeper
          round about eleven thirty...where
          is this bag now?


                    **BRADERICK**
          ...I don't know nuffing about no
          black Gucchi handbag stolen from
          the riverside this morning


                    **HOLMES**
          I do not recall saying anything
          of the location nor description

Braderick shifts his feet and looks the ground uncomfortable
realising his mistake.

                    **BRADERICK**
          ...dammit

                    **HOLMES**
There you have it Watson
confirmation we have the right
man...so can we sort this between
us here and now or do we need to
involve the Police Mr Braderick
"Deferred Prison Sentence"
Theobald


                    **BRADERICK**
You can't prove anything...a case
of mistaken identity, you don't
have one bit a proof


                    **HOLMES**
He is of course correct Watson I
do not have a singular piece of
proof...

Braderick sneers triumphant.

                    **HOLMES**
I in fact have TWO pieces on top
of your round about confession
just then...shall I take you
through them? I think I
shall...first off we already know
you are the one whom was painting
Rabbi Coleslaws house, a
distinctive choice of red I will
add..."Strawberry Scarlett "


                                                    CUT TO


**FLASHBACK**


                    rabbi coleslaw
...though I would be interested if
anyone was selling Strawberry
Scarlett paint tins ...I need some
more for I am needing to finish
painting my house with this...it is
hard to get hold of...not the most
popular of choices...I had a boy
for free! Community Service...


                                                    FADE BACK
                                                    TO SCENE

                        71

                    **HOLMES**
          It would have been easy for tiny
          amounts of the paint to have been
          transferred during the painting
          process and remain there for some
          time…so when you grabbed at Miss
          Blake's scarf when you went to
          snatch the bag you left traces of
          the paint upon the scarf

                                                    CUT TO


**flashback**



                    HOLMES
          Not blood…red…paint…ahah in fact
          studying it closer…Scarlett

                                                    FADE BACK
                                                    TO SCENE




                    **HOLMES**
          This was confirmed to be the
          distinct paint when I cross-
          referenced the flakes on the
          scarf to the paint

                                                    CUT TO


**FLASHBACK**

                    RABBI COLESLAW
          No no…it was…it was "Scarlett
          Strawberry"… here here I still
          have the colour chart from the
          DIY store.

Holmes takes the card and holds it to light smiling slyly.

                    holmes
          Perfect match…

                                                    FADE BACK
                                                    TO SCENE

                    **BRADERICK**
That's not enough to prove it to
the law


                    **HOLMES**
By itself of course not…this was
just the icing of the cake that
led me to connect it all
together, my main clue came from
the very fact there were NO
foreign fingerprints upon Miss
Blake's scarf despite you
reaching with a bare hand…

                                        CUT TO


***FLASHBACK***


                    holmes
…there are 3 sets of clearly
identified finger prints upon
this scarf, Miss Blakes, Mine and
your own…there is a 4th set of
markings but I do not believe
them to be fingerprints…to
blurred and no ringlet patten
upon them…


                    watson
But…he grabbed it Holmes…I saw
him…with his bare hands…he
grabbed it…I am so sure of it


                                        FADE BACK
                                        TO SCENE

                    **HOLMES**
Now the only way to have no trace
of fingerprints at all…
would be if one had them burnt
off…it is common practice in
Mafia and Triad circles to avoid
finger print detection…

                    **BRADERICK**
    BUT...


                    **HOLMES**
    BUT nothing Mr Theobald! We also
    know you recently suffered an
    accident with a blow torch whilst
    painting Rabbi Coleslaws house...an
    accident which resulted in burnt
    hands

                                        CUT TO


**FLASHBACK**


                    WATSON
    But as he was doing the stripping
    and repainting of a Rabbi Leaders
    house the blow torch backfired
    causing severe burning to his
    hands and he fell off the ladder
    too...poor lad

                                        FADE OUT

                    **HOLMES**
    You effectively have no
    fingerprints, so of course I
    could never trace you in an index
    of them...instead you leave a
    blurred mark upon whatever you
    may touch. Which accounts for the
    fourth stumpy set of imprints
    upon the scarf...so really it could
    not be simpler, I needed someone
    who had come into contact with
    some "Strawberry Scarlett"
    paint...was likely to have a
    criminal background and had no
    finger prints...

Braderick sighs dejectedly realising he has been beaten and
stares to the ground.

                    **BRADERICK**
    ...you said we didn't have to
    involve Police...what do I have to
    do?

                        74

                    **HOLMES**
          The return of the bag if you will
          be so kind...*all* its contents and
          replace the mints you have
          clearly taken from it which I can
          smell upon your breath, Miss
          Blake has a very distinctive
          brand "Glacier Snow Mints" did
          you know Watson I have become
          somewhat of an expert of the
          identification of mints...I am
          thinking of writing a monograph
          on the subject

Braderick tests his breath on his hand looking guilty.

                    **BRADERICK**
          All right, all right...yeah you got
          me give me five minutes and I'll
          go home and get the bag...

Watson leans in closer and hisses in his ear.

                    **WATSON**
          I think I should come with you,
          how do we know you will return...

                    **BRADERICK**
          Well you have me over a barrel
          aintcha mate...one word to the
          Police and it will be
          bye bye deferred prison sentence

                    **HOLMES**
          Let him go Watson,we shall wait
          right here...do not betray my trust
          or your stretch of freedom will
          end very shortly and very sharply

                    **BRADERICK**
          I won't you can trust me...I'll get
          it...be as quick as I can

Watson releases his grip and allows Braderick to scurry away
down the alleyway glancing back occasionally in panicked fear.

                    **WATSON**
See that you are…

Holmes watches Braderick as he limps into the distance and is
joined by Watson at his side.

                    **WATSON**
Holmes…why is it that you can
have catchphrases and I cannot?


                    **HOLMES**
Catchphrases? What are you
talking about I have no such need
for such things, this is just
Miss Blake poisoning you with her
modern television speak is it
not?


                    **WATSON**
"The Games Afoot" "It's my
business to know what other
people don't know" "Bring your
service revolver"


                    **HOLMES**
…those are just things I have
said…once or twice at the most


                    **WATSON**
"When you eliminate the
impossible whatever remains no
matter how improbable must be the
truth"


                    **HOLMES**
Yes thank you Watson


                    **WATSON**
"Immediately if not sooner"

HOLMES
Yes THANK you Watson…

FADE OUT


## SCENE 11
## INT: HOLMES/WATSON LIVING ROOM

Miss Blake is curled up on the sofa looking gloomy and lethargic.

*SFX*
*Sound of footsteps*


Watson and Holmes enter the room slowly. Holmes holds the handbag in front of him and clears his throat causing Miss Blake to stir slightly and glance over at them.

HOLMES
There you are Miss Blake…one
handbag as promised

Miss Blake leaps to her feet in excitement and rushes over.

MISS BLAKE
OH MY GAWD! THANK YOU MR HOLMES!

She hugs Holmes who tries to pull away but awkwardly accepts it. She then breaks off and clinches Watson who is surprised but appears to enjoy it a great deal more.

MISS BLAKE
And Doctor Watson! THANK YOU… OH
you've been such a star to me
today…

Miss Blake pulls away and starts rooting through handbag.

MISS BLAKE
It's all here, my phone, my comb
and my lip stick and my diary and
my eyebrow pencil and my
mints…and my compact mirror…and…


HOLMES
I am only so sorry Miss Blake
that…we were *unable* to retrieve
the bag of clothes from your
shopping trip for us

CUT TO

77

EXT: ALLY WAY

Braderick stands opposite Holmes and Watson. Holmes is holding
Miss Blakes handbag and still dressed in his old woman
disguise. Braderick sulkily hands over a bag with clothes
spilling over the top

                    BRADERICK
          Here…these are the clothes I took
          when I stole the handbag…figured
          you would want them back

Holmes takes the bag and looks through it warily.

                    HOLMES
          Watson…are these the clothes Miss
          Blake bought for us to start
          wearing?


                    WATSON
          Yes that's them…


                    HOLMES
   …mm…


                    WATSON
          Come on Holmes they are
          not…THAT…bad…really…


                    HOLMES
          Watson look me in the eye and
          tell me your happy not one item
          in this bag appears to be tweed


                    WATSON
          Well I…its…you…just…I mmm…


                    HOLMES
          Thought as much…RIGHT well here
          you Mr. Theobald…a present for
          your honestly…well eventual
          honesty

He shoves the bag back into Bradericks hands who seems
baffled.

                          **BRADERICK**
               ...but

                          **HOLMES**
               NEVER Seen them...

                                                      CUT TO


INT: HOLMES/WATSON LIVING ROOM


                          **HOLMES**
               For you see sadly the clothes had
               already been sold on by the time
               we got there...

                          **MISS BLAKE**
               Aw...well that's a shame but I do
               have my handbag back and that's
               what really matters

                          **WATSON**
               Though I expect you are itching
               to go off on another trip to clad
               us out again...

                          **MISS BLAKE**
               No

Holmes and Watson exchange looks of bafflement.

                          **H+W**
               NO?????

                          **MISS BLAKE**
               No after today and my ordeal...I
               think I am going to have a rest
               from shopping...at least till
               tomorrow...unless I hear there's a
               sale of course...

Holmes shakes head and rolls eyes to Watson.

                         HOLMES
            ...of course



                         MISS BLAKE
            BUT Oh thank you again really
            this means so much to me, I am so
            blessed to know you Mr Holmes and
            you Doctor Watson...ever since I
            met you...it just seems to have
            brought me nothing but good
            things...


                                        FADE OUT



SCENE 12
INT:DUNGEON BASEMENT

MADELINE CHAMBERS sits at a black cloth covered table; red
candles are lit and flickering away. The table is covered in
jewels and artefacts.

She has a deerstalker hat clutched together in her hands
screwing it up furiously.

Braderick stands a few feet away from her hands behind back
nervously.

                         MADELINE
            I want him stopped...I want his
            stupid doctor stopped...I want his
            dippy housekeeper stopped...THAT
            SHERLOCK HOLMES HAS BEEN NOTHING
            BUT TROUBLE


She throws the deerstalker across the room narrowly avoiding
Braderick's face.

                         BRADERICK
            I don't think his friend can be
            that stupid he is a doctor and
            all...I think the exams are really
            pretty tough and


                           80

                    MADELINE
          SHUT UP…HOW can I ever get to be
          a leader of a recognizable Super
          Villain League if I can't even
          dominate running petty crime
          brackets…


                    BRADERICK
...sorry Boss


                    MADELINE
          YOU SHOULD BE SORRY…I put in
          loads of work for those bag
          snatches…coordinating the areas
          and times to strike so as no
          Police presence would be about.
          It was supposed to be simple, my
          workers on the other hand ARENT
          MEANT TO BE SIMPLE…I *wanted*
          women's handbags…do you know how
          much stuff we keep in handbags?
          They are like mini goldmines


                    BRADERICK
          Well I may not have got the
          handbag but look I did get the
          clothes bag still…

Braderick nervously steps forward and pushes the bag of
clothes Holmes let him take back.

Madeline scowls and begins searching through it.

                    MADELINE
          Right…well don't want that…that's
          disgusting…don't want this…SEE
          this is no good to me…oooh other
          than the cashmere sweater…that's
          to die for…I think I'll keep
          that…BUT THE REST…its a couple of
          quid down the market at best


                    BRADERICK
          Sorry Boss…he was just too smart


Madeline's head turns and she scowls.

                              MADELINE
               SHUT UP! You think I don't know
               that

She picks up a diary from in front of her.

                              MADELINE [CONT]
               Twice before we have crossed
               paths and he has been a nuisance,
               first on September 26th 2010…when
               my stupid half sister came to him
               to get Daddies antique watch back
               that I had painstakingly set her
               up to have lose…HE managed to
               figure out it was all my
               doing…four month stretch in
               prison thank you very much Mr
               Holmes…

She flicks the diary a few pages forward.

                              MADELINE
               Then again, on March 3rd 2011…I
               had successfully pulled off a
               bank raid for 50,000 pounds…BUT
               lo and behold he and a Baker
               Street brat turn up and very near
               foiled me, the only reason I got
               away was through stabbing him…but
               that was far to close for comfort
               for my liking

She flicks backwards a few pages and scowls.

                              MADELINE
               And now THIS! It just FEELS like
               he is always in my way ohh…I
               don't know…it's as if I have
               lived a past life and…and…he was
               there messing things up for me
               then…


                              BRADERICK
               Eh?


                              MADELINE
               Oh forget it I don't know…where
               did he even come from anyway? I
               had never even heard of him
               before…it's like he …appeared out
               of thin air like…magic…

She flicks her hair before she picks up her phone and dials a
number.

                        MADELINE
                It's Chambers…now listen I want
                24/7 recon on Mr. Sherlock Holmes
                and Doctor John Watson…I want
                full intelligence reports on
                their comings and goings…I want
                their backgrounds…anything you
                can find on them I want to know…


She stretches her hand out to examine her fingernails.

                        MADELINE
                He might appear to be on the side
                of angels…but there must be
                something about his past
                I can use against him……every
                family has skeletons in the
                closet

Madeline puts her phone down and leans forward slightly
grinning maliciously with a far away look in her eye.

                        MADELINE
                Sherlock Holmes will curse the
                day he ever crossed swords
                with…The…Red…Headed…League…

She smirks to herself confidently seemingly lost in her own
thoughts. Braderick unfolds his arms and thinks about this for
a few seconds before nervously piping up.

                        BRADERICK
                But I'm really more strawberry
                blonde Miss…

Madeline turns to him and frowns at this suggestion before she
spits out aggressively.

                        MADELINE
                What? Oh…for goodness sake…I'll
                dye it!




Braderick looks crestfallen at this and nervously twiddles his
hair.

Madeline turns away and crosses her arms again staring
intently in the darkness of the dungeon lost in deep
contemplation for her revenge.


**END**

<u>NO PLACE LIKE HOLMES</u>
<u>SERIES 3 EPISODE 2</u>
<u>REIGN WILL FALL</u>

ORIGINAL RUN 1ST NOVEMBER - 17TH NOVEMBER 2012 (5 PARTS).

<u>CAST</u>

SHERLOCK HOLMES.................................ROSS K FOAD
DR JOHN H.WATSON...........................MIKE ARCHER
MISS CHRISTINE BLAKE..............................TAMZIN DUNSTONE
MISS REBECCA CONSTANCE.........................ANGELA HOLMES
MISS MADELINE CHAMBERS.........................KELSEY WILLIAMS
BRADERICK THEOBALD.....................BARNABY TWYMAN
MISS KATRINA BLISS....................................VICTORIA-JANE APPLETON
MR JAMES PHILLIMORE..................................GENE FOAD
MR.TRISTAN QUICK...........................................PAUL BALLARD
CORRUPT COUNCIL OFFICIAL(VOICE) FIONA JANE-BROWN

85

SCENE 1:
INT: MADELINE'S DUNGEON

Open to find MADELINE CHAMBERS sitting down at her table in
her cellar dungeon. Her mobile phone to her ear with one hand,
the other slams the table in front of her in rage, BRADERICK
THEOBALD stands by upright looking on nervously.

                    MADELINE
          What do you mean NOTHING!


                    WOMANS V/O
          I mean there is nothing I…


Madeline slams the table with her fist again.


                    MADELINE
          There HAS to be something…what is
          the bloody point of having
          someone corrupt in the council if
          you cant find what I need? Are
          you sure that you have checked
          ALL your records? Housing? Tax?
          Parking? Look I'd even take
          library card details at this
          stage just …tell me
          SOMETHING…ANYTHING???


                    WOMAN V/O
          Miss Chambers I am sorry but as
          far as we are concerned and
          please remember, I have looked
          over records dating back ten
          years…but as far as this council
          is concerned Mr Sherlock Holmes
          and Doctor Watson do not
          exist…your other enquiry
          though…the housekeeper Miss
          Blake? There are plenty of
          records for her…


                    MADELINE
          Tut…the dippy one? Well that's
          better than nothing…fine…encrypt
          and email them over

Madeline rolls her eyes and puts phone back on the table.
Her mouth twitches anxiously as she grinds her teeth and drums
the table with her fingers.

                    MADELINE
          I knew it Braderick I knew it…those
          two are hiding something…they have
          to be…they must be fake names! They
          have lived in this town for at
          least two years…how can there be no
          official records of them in the
          council? What are they hiding? I
          want to know…I need to know


                    BRADERICK
          I get that they are a nuisance to
          you and all miss…and your life
          would be easier without the worry
          of them foiling your plans…but what
          makes you so sure there is
          something dodgy about them? I mean
          they do make a living out of
          stopping dodgy people…surely that
          don't make sense…


                    MADELINE
          …your very naïve Braderick…but
          that's what I like about you… you
          believe anything your told


Braderick considers this for a second before he nods
enthusiastic.

                    BRADERICK
          Do I? Oh ok


                    MADELINE
          And I can't explain exactly why I
          feel it…but I just do…there is
          something deep down inside me that
          just…well that just knows ok!

                              BRADERICK
                    Oh right…maybe its love


Madeline turns to face him and spits out disgusted.


                              MADELINE
                         LOVE!?


                              BRADERICK
                    Yeah…love is a feeling that can't
                    really be explained. So maybe
                    that is it, maybe you love
                    Sherlock Holmes?

The flames rises in Madeline's eye as she is about as she
begins to lose her temper only for her phone to start
vibrating causing her to turn her attention onto that instead.


                              MADELINE
                    BRADERICK…I…oh………perfect…here
                    take a good look at this photo,
                    this is the woman who is going to
                    help us bring about the fall of
                    Sherlock Holmes and Doctor Watson
                    and then nothing can stop my
                    reign as the worlds greatest
                    super villain taking place…


Braderick looks at the photo then seems slightly taken aback
as he shakes head.


                              BRADERICK
                    But that's the house keeper…we
                    stole the bag from her…oh no I
                    don't think she will want to help
                    us


                              MADELINE
                    Idiot…she doesn't *know* she is
                    going to help us

                         BRADERICK
              But you just said she…


                         MADELINE
              *Braderick*…just let me do the
              thinking…

Braderick goes to open his mouth in protest.

                         MADELINE
              AND…the talking…AND I thought I
              told you to dye your hair


                         BRADERICK
              …Well I tried but there were all
              these different…boxes…and the
              colours…and it was all really
              confusing…and then…and then…

Madeline throws arms up in defeat and lets out a sigh
returning to browsing her diary as Braderick returns to his
original position of nervously twiddling his hair and glancing
around the dungeon.


                                           FADE OUT



**SCENE 2**
**INT: HOLMES LIVING ROOM**

A dark haired woman in her late 20's wearing glasses, high
heels and a tight fitting black dress sits on the sofa
nervously tapping her fingers upon her coat which she is
clutching close to her.

                         *SFX:*
                 *FOOTSTEPS APPROACHING*

Watson enters the living room then pauses slightly surprised
by the figure on the sofa but quickly composes himself and
steps forward to speak to her.


                         WATSON
              Oh good morning there…are you
              waiting to see Mr. Ho…

She gets herself up off the sofa quickly and strides straight
over to him cutting his speech of mid flow.

                         MISS CONSTANCE
        Yes you Mr Holmes…your house
        keeper said I could wait I hope
        you don't mind, I have this
        problem that really requires your
        immediate attention, please say
        that you can come? I have read
        all about what you can do in
        those brilliant stories Doctor
        Watson writes for the newspapers


                         WATSON
        Oh but I am afraid I am not
        Mr…brilliant stories you say?


                         MISS CONSTANCE
        Yes ever so…

Watson appears rather pleased with this and steps a few paces
forward while mulling this over.

                         WATSON
        Mmm so what is it you err like
        about them?


                         MISS CONSTANCE
        Everything really…the mystery,
        the action, the excitement…


                         WATSON
        So you don't think perhaps they
        are too "Romanticized" or
        fanciful do you?


                         MISS CONSTANCE
        No not at all

Watson smiles then steps forward closer to her and begins to
speak in a hushed voice.

                         WATSON
        Ahah…well you don't think you
        could repeat that again do you
        when Mr Hol…

                    MISS CONSTANCE
          Though I do have to say I am not
          sure how you put up with that Dr.
          Watson…he seems a bit of a
          bumbler!

Watson shakes his head unsure he has heard correctly then
becomes very peeved.

                       WATSON
          A bit of a bumbler???

Before he is able to correct her HOLMES enters and pushes past
the two of them to go look out of French window.

                       HOLMES
          Ah Good morning Watson…you
          haven't seen my other deerstalker
          have you? Must have mislaid it
          somewhere ah well…I advise you
          wear your wet weather clothes if
          your going out because it is
          quite simply foul out there

Miss Constance watches in slight awe as well as confusion as
he then suddenly spins on his heels pointing his long steeped
together fingers at her.

                       HOLMES
          AHAH! *You* must be Miss
          Constance…my housekeeper informed
          me you wished to consult me on
          something urgently

                    MISS CONSTANCE
          Wait…YOUR Mr.Holmes?

                       HOLMES
          …yes?

                    MISS CONSTANCE
          Oh but then who…

She points to Watson who has abruptly and grumpily pushed past
to take position at the end of the room.

                       WATSON
          I shall just bumble over here
          until I am needed shall I?

**MISS CONSTANCE**

Oh...dear I did not mean...it is
just...I ooh...

Miss Constance seems distraught and begins to move forward to
him to apologize but is steered away by Holmes swiftly seating
her upon the sofa.

**HOLMES**

Never mind him Miss Constance
...now please sit and explain the
panic that has caused you to act
with such haste you were unable
to even find time to actually put
on your coat before you fled from
your headmistress post at the
highly respectable Bruce Stock
academy

**MISS CONSTANCE**

Yes...I...oh you have read about me
in some articles in the local
paper then?

**HOLMES**

Unless you have appeared in some
sensational murder story or the
classified ads I very much doubt
I have...the former being
particularly unlikely as you
would not be here in front of me
today...that being said I can
recall two notable
"resurrections" that have
occurred within history following
the subjects supposedly
succumbing to death

**WATSON**

Yes and one of them significantly
closer to Holmes you might say...

Holmes turns to face Watson who is leaning against the
doorway.

**HOLMES**

What was that Watson? You will
have to speak up you are mumbling

Watson becomes flustered and indignant to this shaking his head and muttering under his breath.

                    **WATSON**
          Oh so now I am bumbling AND
          mumbling...even better


                    **HOLMES**
          Pray excuse my colleague here
          rain upsets him so...but back to
          your paper question Miss
          Constance no no...the fact I know
          you were in rush, you did not
          even take the time to place your
          coat on despite the terrible
          weather other matters clearly
          pressing


                 **MISS CONSTANCE**
          Oh...yes it must have slipped my
          mind...but my job?

Holmes examines his fingernails stretching his hand out almost bored upon explaining such simplicity.

                    **HOLMES**
          Relatively simple, you have
          splashes of distinctive green
          claymore mud upon your ankles.
          The only place near here with
          such deposits is in Chislehurst
          way, Chislehurst way is a
          relatively private stretch
          trekked only by keen ramblers and
          those attending the near by
          private academy...going on your
          smart dress style I put your
          reason being the latter not the
          former...which also brings us to
          your reason for being at the
          academy...

He narrows his eyes slightly as he eyes her up and down as if scanning her. Miss Constance cocks her head slightly to side bewildered.

                    **HOLMES**
          Too old to be a student...therefore
          a working position...

there is an air of authority and
confidence to you, which would
not be the case if you were a
mere teacher aid or trampled upon
trainee…the only option left…the
Headmistress

                    MISS CONSTANCE
        …Wow…ok you are as good as the
        stories say you are…

Holmes frowns and grimaces slightly.

                    HOLMES
        No I am not actually, *he*
        exaggerates them…

He waves a hand flippantly at Watson.

                    HOLMES
        BUT if are only here to discuss
        "the stories" you are better off
        speaking with Doctor Watson than
        myself

                    WATSON
        Oh we've already had THAT
        conversation Holmes…most
        enlightening…

Miss Constance averts eyes onto the ground and rubs neck
uncomfortable.

                    MISS CONSTANCE
        Erhum…

Holmes looks back and forth between them slightly unsure of
the awkwardness.

                    HOLMES
        Ok? So Miss Constance…your
        problem? Spare no details

                    MISS CONSTANCE
          Yes…look I will tell you now I
          have come to you and not the
          Police…I know you will act with
          discretion. And I really do not
          want this to get out for the sake
          of the Academies reputation and I
          only recently have got this
          position as headmistress, well
          the founders will not look too
          kindly on me if they find out…


                    WATSON
          Find out what exactly?


                    MISS CONSTANCE
          There has been a theft of a very
          significant amount of cash from
          the academy petty cash strong
          hold box this morning…

Holmes holds his hand out indicating her to pause.

                    HOLMES
          Miss Constance I do not mean to
          interrupt your flow but surely
          that is a contradiction…a *petty*
          strong hold cash box which
          contained a "significant amount
          of cash"
          You are an academy…you do not
          make cash sales I imagine and
          surely your term fees are paid in
          advance via cheque?
          So why would there have been so
          much in there

Miss Constance grins sheepishly.

                    MISS CONSTANCE
          Ah yes…that's the other little
          thing I hope I can count on your
          discretion for Mr. Holmes…the
          cash was in there to be used to
          pay for a school trip next month
          to Switzerland, and well we kind
          of got a no tax cash discount
          deal from the holiday company…

Holmes raises an eyebrow but makes no more of this and
continues as if it had never been spoken.

                    HOLMES
At what time was the cash
withdrawn and deposited in this
box?


                  MISS CONSTANCE
I withdrew it from the bank at
one o'clock…by the time I
returned and had deposited it in
the strong hold box it would have
been around half past two, I
returned this morning entered my
office at eight this morning and
to my horror saw the box opened
with the cash gone


                    HOLMES
I see…so the only people who
would have been aware the cash
was to be withdrawn and within
that would have been?


                  MISS CONSTANCE
The members of staff who were
going on the trip…Tristan Quick
the P.E teacher and Katrina Bliss
the librarian


                    HOLMES
You have reasons to suspect their
characters?


                  MISS CONSTANCE
I really do not want too but I
have little choice…Mr. Quick has
had some debt problems that much
I do know, and then Miss Bliss is
leaving us within a month to get
married…she is starting a new
position as head librarian at a
university in Australia

Holmes ponders upon this rubbing chin deep in thought.
His eyes begin to show a sigh of flare and excitement.

                              **HOLMES**
                    ...so a potential little nest egg
                    to enable her to settle down
                    hmmm...Miss Constance...I would very
                    much like to help you and I
                    believe I can...

He turns on his heels with lightening quick speed and points
to Watson still lingering in the doorway.

                              **HOLMES**
                    WATSON! Will you be joining me?
                    Best get our hats if we do the
                    weather sounds atrocious still


                              **WATSON**
                    Well I might just "bumble" along
                    if Miss Constance does not mind
                    too much

Miss Constance crosses the room and holds her hands clasped
together pleading.

                          **MISS CONSTANCE**
                    Oh please Doctor...I didn't mean
                    it...please won't you come too...I
                    want the full package Mr. Holmes
                    *and* Doctor Watson...

She reaches for his arm slowly rubbing her hand along it in an
increasingly seductive manner.

                          **MISS CONSTANCE**
                    It would not be the same with out
                    the faithful, strong, silent...sexy
                    sidekick

Watson blushes and stutters.

                              **WATSON**
                    ...Well when you put it that way


                              **HOLMES**
                    Excellent...you can fill us in on
                    some of the finer points on the
                    way Miss Constance


                          **MISS CONSTANCE**
                    Yes of course...err I couldn't
                    borrow a brolly could I?

She peers out of the French windows concerned at the teeming
rain.

                    WATSON
          Oh I am sure Miss Blake has one
          does she not Holmes?


                    HOLMES
          I am sure she has several of
          varying styles and electric
          colours...we can pick one up on the
          way out...NOW let us move out
          immediately if not sooner for
          time is of the essence and the
          game is indeed afoot!

He grabs his cane off the table and strides out followed by
Miss Constance as Watson slowly tags on behind.


                    WATSON
          And here come the catchphrases...

Holmes spins around to face Watson again.

                    HOLMES
          What was that Watson? You will
          have to speak up...you were
          mumbling again


                    WATSON
          Nothing...nothing...will you require
          me to bring my service revolver
          perhaps?


                    HOLMES
          Service revolver? Watson we are
          going to a school...think of the
          children...SAFETY!!!!

Holmes shakes his head and whispers to Miss Constance in a
stage style manner.

                    HOLMES
          Sorry I do apologize...he can be
          quite the bumbler sometimes

Holmes strides out followed by a giggling Miss Constance.

                          WATSON
            …Bumbler!??

Watson shakes his head grits his teeth then follows on after
them.

                                          FADE OUT


## SCENE 3
## EXT:GROUNDS OF ACADEMY

Holmes Watson and Miss Constance all huddle along slowly under
a large umbrella held up by Miss Constance as the rain
continues to teem down.


                          HOLMES
                 So Miss Constance is the strong
                 hold boxes entry by means of a
                 key? Alternatively, it is of the
                 tumbler lock variety and if so
                 who had the number combination?


                       MISS CONSTANCE
                 It's combination, both Mr. Quick
                 and Miss Bliss knew the code


                          WATSON
                 Could any one else have known of
                 this number?


                       MISS CONSTANCE
                 Well it is possible I guess…

Holmes snorts and shakes his head.

                          HOLMES
                 Guessing is a filthy habit…please
                 refrain from doing so further,
                 now then…come on Watson you
                 remember Afghanistan ONWARDS
                 quick march!

Holmes begins to stride out fast away from the umbrella
leaving a concerned Watson to call out after him.

                    **WATSON**
          Oh Holmes…Holmes where are you
          going? It is still raining


                    **HOLMES**
          Your observation skills are
          getting better Watson


                    **WATSON**
          …If you catch pneumonia it will
          be your own doing and then I am
          not going to stand around playing
          nurse to you as a resident
          patient

Holmes continues to stride quickly and merely shouts back.

                    **HOLMES**
          Good! I abhor mollycoddling


                    **WATSON**
          I shall ask Miss Blake to do so
          instead, she will be on strict
          instructions to be by your
          bedside morning, noon and night
          and I KNOW how much you enjoyed
          the last time

                                        CUT TO



INT: HOLMES/WATSON LIVING ROOM

MISS BLAKE is fussing over a dressing gown clad Holmes sitting
on the sofa as she is trying to tuck a blanket over him
despite his obvious resistance.

                    **MISS BLAKE**
          So how are you feeling today Mr.
          Holmes?


                    **HOLMES**
          Well I…

Miss Blake shoves a thermometer in his mouth.

                    **MISS BLAKE**
          That's nice…you know I wouldn't
          have minded doing this nursing
          stuff full time for real and I
          would have!  If it wasn't for the
          long hours, the lack of social
          life, the low pay, the uniforms
          not being the right colour OH and
          I don't like the smell of
          hospitals…OH and then there's the
          sick people I would probably get
          all sorts of diseases…OH You know
          my Auntie Pat?

Holmes spits out the thermometer.

                    **HOLMES**
          …Oh yes, I have heard all about
          Auntie Pat…

Miss Blake puts the thermometer back in his mouth.

                    **MISS BLAKE**
          Right well she went into hospital
          in 1994 for an ingrown toenail
          and sat next to a pregnant woman
          in the waiting room…3 weeks later
          she keeps being sick and being
          sick…so she went back only to
          find out she was pregnant
          herself! Coincidence? I think
          not…see told you place is full of
          it

Holmes spits out his thermometer once again.

                    **HOLMES**
          So what part of the profession
          *does* attract you then?

                    **MISS BLAKE**
          Uh? George Clooney obviously

Miss Blake shoves the thermometer in his mouth once again as
he crosses his arms silently fuming.

                    **MISS BLAKE**
          Mr. Holmes are you all right? The
          thermometers rising very quickly
          now…

                          101

EXT: ACADEMY GROUNDS

Fresh from the memory of such a harrowing experience Holmes dejectedly sighs and shakes his head stamping backwards until he is under the umbrella once more with Watson and Miss Constance.

                        HOLMES
             ...Sigh...


                        HOLMES
             There...can we go now?


                        WATSON
             There's a good chap...


                        HOLMES
             I DIDN'T enjoy it last time by
             the way


                        WATSON
             That is because you never gave
             her a chance

They continue to bicker over this as they walk into the Academy's entrance and the rain continues to fall at an increasing fast pace.


SCENE 4
EXT: OUTSIDE HOLMES HOUSE

Madeline scurries along the pathway to Holmes house dressed in a large flowing pink dress, long pink heels and oversized sunglasses.

She is clutching a candy cane and an overly large handbag to her side as she waves for Braderick to follow her.

Braderick is dressed in tight white polo shirt, white chino trousers, large sunglasses and clutching a camera bag to his chest.

                        MADELINE
              Come on…hurry up…

She raps at the door with the candy cane and they wait. Miss Blake comes out the house and answers door glancing between the two slightly unsure about the strange couple.

                        MISS BLAKE
              …Hello?


                        MADELINE
              HELLO…I'm Senior Gossip Editor
              Candy Kane and this is my
              photographer Freddie Flash …we're
              from…HELLO

Miss Blake is puzzled at first but then it dawns on her and becomes very excited.

                        MISS BLAKE
              Hello? …OH…HELLO!!!


                        MADELINE
              Yes…so we were wondering if you…


                        MISS BLAKE
              COME IN!!!

Miss Blake grabs Madeline and ushers her inside quickly


                                          FADE OUT
                                          FADE IN



INT:HOLMES LIVING ROOM

Miss Blake ushers Madeline and Braderick through to the living room and onto the sofa before they even have a chance to protest.

She then pulls up a chair from the table setting directly in front and sits her self-down excitedly.

>                    **MISS BLAKE**
> HELLO is my all time fave
> magazine ever OH It is such an
> honour to have you here...OH can I
> get you anything tea, coffee,
> freshly squeezed orange juice or
> maybe champagne? OR something to
> eat perhaps like A-Pain-Au
> Chocolate? Strawberries and
> Cream? Ferro Rochehe? These are
> all things we always have very
> regularly here of course

>                    **MADELINE**
> Of course

>                    **BRADERICK**
> Well I wouldn't mind a...

Madeline elbows him to be quiet then smiles again.

>                    **MISS BLAKE**
> Now err...why exactly are you here
> anyway?

>                    **MADELINE**
> We...

>                    **MISS BLAKE**
> Don't I know you? Your very
> familiar...what did you say your
> name was again?

Madeline and Braderick exchange worried expressions before Madeline waves her candy cane again excitedly and enthusiastic.

>                    **MADELINE**
> Candy Kane...and I am sure you do
> recognize me...any ones who is
> *somebody* KNOWS Candy Kane...you are
> a *somebody* aren't you?

                    MISS BLAKE
OH YES…Yes absolutely
definitely…Its all coming back
now…Posh and Becks last party?
That is probably where we
passed…wasn't he a scream? She's
a bit dowdy though…


                    MADELINE
Err ah yes Posh and Becks…that
will be when you saw me

Miss Blake nods satisfied despite the fact she made up the
event she claims to know Candy from but then turns her
attention to Braderick looking at him slightly suspiciously.

                    MISS BLAKE
But your kinda familiar too where
might I have seen you before?


                    MADELINE
Err YES…you probably have seen
him at one of the many parties
you no doubt attend…on hand to
bag all the exclusives…err poor
choice of words there…anyway! He
is very dedicated


Madeline pats him on the back and he nods enthusiastic.


                    BRADERICK
I sleep on Katy Perry's doorstep!


                    MADELINE
HAHA…yes…umm but now the reason
we are here today well
Christine…can I call you
Christine?


Miss Blake looks blank and looks from to the other.

                    MISS BLAKE
          …you can but I don't know why you
          would?



                    MADELINE
          Because it's your name…?



Madeline and Braderick look down at her notebook puzzled
trying to find where they wrote her name down.



                    MISS BLAKE
          …OH yes of course it is OH GAWD
          my memory…sieve! Sorry YEAH call
          me what you like…Mr. Holmes
          doesn't really use first
          names…John doesn't mind as much
          but it's just the way things are
          in our house really



                    MADELINE
          Oh that Mr. Holmes…you must have
          so many stories



                    MISS BLAKE
          Oh DO I!

Madeline smiles slyly to Braderick and begins twirling her
silver fountain pen.

                    MADELINE
          This is why we at HELLO want to
          do an article on you

Miss Blake places her face in her hands and lets out a shriek
of excitement.

                    MISS BLAKE
          O…M…G

                    **MADELINE**
Yes Mr. Holmes has fast become a
popular but oh SO mysterious
figure and you are the closest
know woman to him…so we know our
readers would love to hear all
about the woman who keeps Holmes
home


                    **MISS BLAKE**
This is so exciting I have waited
my whole life for an article in a
celeb mag…will there be photos
and everything?

Miss Blake jumps out of her chair to her feet.


                    **MISS BLAKE**
Let me go change, I have about
twenty outfits that I have picked
out encase this ever happened so
I will show you and you can
decide which one we can go with
OOH maybe we can use them all?
Give you a selection of photos;
now that would be good wouldn't
it! OH then there's make up cos
each outfit has a different set
to compliment it and OH do you
think I can go get a pedicure
before we begin?

Madeline looks at her watch uneasy while Braderick is looking
petrified by her level of enthusiasm.

                    **MADELINE**
Uh well…we really don't have the
time for all of that, besides I
am sure Flash can…just air brush
it


                    **MISS BLAKE**
Oh, right…well just the clothes
then!


                    **MADELINE**
Err…no no he can err do all of
that digitally too…he's amazing

Miss Blake returns and sits back down in her chair staring in awe of him.

                    MISS BLAKE
          Really? Wow I did not know you
          could do that now…


                    BRADERICK
          Neither did I?

Madeline scowls and gently nudges him with her elbow.

                    BRADERICK
          OH yeah I do it all the time
          love…it's a snap…snap…camera
          thing…ahahah don't mind me love
          I'm just mad as a box of frogs


                    MADELINE
          Yeah alright don't over do it,
          SO Christine…tell us about your
          life and err any details about
          Mr. Holmes you might want to
          throw in well just feel free, I
          am sure we can put them to good
          use…


                                        FADE OUT


SCENE 5
INT: STAFF ROOM

Holmes and Watson enter the staff room following on behind
Miss Constance; the table is covered with papers teacups,
tennis balls, exercise jotters, a packet of brown hair dye and
various stationary items.


Holmes eye roams around until it settles upon a certificate he
picks up and examines with considerable interest.

                    HOLMES
          Mm…look at this Watson a 2.1 in
          the field of Theatre Studies,
          admirable Miss Constance…you were
          not then moved to follow a life
          on stage?

MISS CONSTANCE

Well that is a distant dream now
really…so as they say "Those who
can't *do*…teach!"


HOLMES

Surely as Headmistress, you no
longer teach.


MISS CONSTANCE

Umm…I…err…well…no

Holmes presses his tongue against his cheek mildly amused at
Miss Constance's evident embarrassment as Watson takes another
cursory glance around the room at the windows and doors.

WATSON

So Miss Constance…this room is
accessible at all hours then to
anyone who might pass


MISS CONSTNCE

Well yes but it is hardly an
issue…well at least it never used
to be, as we have never had a
problem with theft before

She turns and walks a few paces forward picking up a cached
wooden box and handing it to Holmes.


MISS CONSTANCE

There is the strong hold box

Holmes takes it from her and holds it close to his face before
he runs a hand along the edge of the box.

HOLMES

It does not appear to have been
forced…there are no prizing scuff
marks…no scratches or dents


MISS CONSTANCE

Which means what exactly?

                    HOLMES
It was definitely opened via the
combination lock


                MISS CONSTANCE
Then that means it was Mr. Quick
or Miss Bliss


                    HOLMES
Not necessarily, it means the
perpetrator knew the
combination…but as there is no
apparent sign of a break in at
the door to the academy or any
broken windows, we can safely say
that it is an internal matter

Holmes scans the room with a slightly sly smile upon his face
as Watson gazes puzzled at the strong hold box.

                    WATSON
So what shall we do now Holmes?


                    HOLMES
Ask and we shall receive
Watson…ask and we shall receive,
least that is the scriptures
instructions are…I would like to
question Mr. Quick and Miss
Bliss, I presume they are aware
of this occurrence?


                MISS CONSTANCE
Yes of course, I spoke to them
both just encase there had been
some horrible mistake but no…they
both seemed mortified by it
naturally…but then they would do
wouldn't they? But someone is
lying


                    HOLMES
Mmm…the question is…who?

                                FADE OUT

SCENE 6
INT: HOLMES/WATSON LIVING ROOM

Open to Miss Blake still seated upon a chair in front of
Madeline and Braderick on the sofa as she rabbits away at
speed much to their bafflement.

                    MISS BLAKE
               …So that's the story of how I got
               my first rabbit or was it the
               second? OH no matter…but to this
               day right, now THIS is funny…my
               Auntie Pat STILL can't even *look*
               at a carrot without breaking into
               a sweat…

Madeline and Braderick exchange a look of bewilderment as
Madeline shrugs.

                    MISS BLAKE
               Which is a shame because she used
               to really like making carrot
               cake…OH but she still makes it
               but with out the carrot…so it
               shouldn't really be called that
               should it? Anyway do you want to
               know about my school days?

Madeline frowns and flicks out her wrist to examine her watch.

                    MADELINE
               Er…no…you're all right…


                    MISS BLAKE
               Oh good because I can't really
               remember much about them…now what
               where we talking about…



                    MADELINE
               Err…



                    MISS BLAKE
               So anyway, back to Mr. Holmes…

At the mention of this, Madeline sits upright attentive
clutching her note pad.

                    MADELINE
               Yes?

111

                    MISS BLAKE
          A lot of people think its all
          robbers and bandits
          that Mr. Holmes stops but it
          isn't no…not always, and I should
          know I help him on a lot of the
          cases, I'm like the "Executive
          Assistant Case Investigator"…I
          should get that as a t-shirt
          shouldn't I? That would be good
          wouldn't it? Anyway, there was
          this one time we stopped a ghost


                    MADELINE
          Wait a ghost? So you are also
          like…Ghostbusters?

Miss Blake claps hands together and shrieks in excitement
causing Braderick and Madeline to flinch slightly.

                    MISS BLAKE
          THAT'S EXACTLY WHAT I SAID!!!! Oh
          you and I are so alike Candy, but
          no Mr. Holmes said we aren't but
          we are really because this one
          client had a ghost NO he thought
          it was a ghost, so we used this
          other ghost to tell us it wasn't
          a ghost and anyway it was peanut
          butter in the end or something

Braderick turns to Madeline shaking his head.


                    BRADERICK
          I am so confused right now


Madeline pats his shoulder sympathetically.


                    MISS BLAKE
          Someone was sleepwalking too…one
          of the ghosts I think

                    **MADELINE**
Clearly yes…um how about family?
I am just so curious about what
kind of family he must be from


                    **MISS BLAKE**
Oh…he doesn't really talk about
them; he can be a bit private
about that


                    **MADELINE**
Really? Why does this not
surprise me…


                    **MISS BLAKE**
He has a brother…I know that cos
he does mention him occasionally.
Does something a bit top secret I
think maybe a spy or something
but I've never met him no…I have
asked but he just says its not
possible…got a funny name
too…Mycroft

Madeline jots this down repeating the name silently as she
does.

                    **MADELINE**
Mycroft…Mycroft Holmes? So…
Mycroft and Sherlock


                    **MISS BLAKE**
Yeah I know…What WERE the family
thinking…but they are French so I
suppose that explains it


                    **BRADERICK**
He's French? He don't sound it

                    **MISS BLAKE**
Well no he wasn't born in France
I don't think, I mean he would be
far more fashion conscious then
wouldn't he! That's another funny
thing about him dresses very old
fashioned…Doctor Watson too…
I wish they wouldn't but I can't
get them to change…I have tried
and tried but nope they will not
do it

Madeline notes this down in her pad slightly puzzled.

                    **MISS BLAKE**
Anyway French is in his blood I
remember he said something about
his Grandmother being sister to
some French artist…no one
important though, I mean you
wouldn't see him in HELLO! Verdy?
Vermin? Venknot?


                    **MADELINE**
Vernet?

Miss Blake shrieks and claps hands together enthusiastic.

                    **MISS BLAKE**
YEAH that's it! Oh you are clever
Candy


                    **MADELINE**
…mm…

                    *SFX*
                 *PHONE RINGS*


Miss Blake glances around and leaps up.

                    **MISS BLAKE**
OH I am so sorry I won't be a
minute…that's probably me Auntie
Pat! She *always* calls at this
time on a Wednesday


                    **BRADERICK**
But it's Tuesday…

Miss Blake waves hand flippantly laughing.

                    **MISS BLAKE**
          Yeah but Auntie Pat won't know
          that!

She strides across the room and picks phone off its cradle
answering it as Madeline and Braderick exchange bewildered
expressions.

                    **MISS BLAKE**
          Hello…OH AUNTIE PAT you'll never
          guess whose here…HELLO…
          …No I know you can hear me I mean
          that's whose here HEL-LO
          …yes I know I've already said
          hello Auntie Pat no don't worry I
          can hear you fine…but that's
          whose here HELLO

Miss Blake continues to try to explain in vain
as Madeline leans it closer to Braderick and whispers pointing
to the notes on her pad.

                    **MADELINE**
          This doesn't make sense…I know
          everything there is to know on
          antiques and rare arts, the
          French artist Vernet died in 1863
          so Mr. Holmes Grandma *couldn't*
          have been his sister

                    **BRADERICK**
          Well…she is completely mad

                    **MADELINE**
          That…or Sherlock Holmes is
          feeding her a pack of lies which
          confirms there is something very
          suspicious about him

They glance towards Miss Blake still on the phone.

                    **MISS BLAKE**
          No Auntie Pat…its HELLO…NO I know
          I keep saying it I've not
          forgotten BUT that's who is
          here…HELLO…NOOO you don't need to
          keep saying hello back to me
          every time…HELLO?

                              BRADERICK
          I'm still going with the
          completely mad theory


                              MISS BLAKE
          HELLO......Noo...HELLO!!!

Madeline raises eyebrows and nods before returning to scribble
down more notes as Miss Blake continues to blither away
endlessly.


                                                  FADE OUT


**SCENE 7**
**EXT:FOOTBALL FIELD**

Watson and Holmes are walking across a field adjacent to the
dressing rooms as Holmes examines a timetable held out in
front of him.

                              HOLMES
                    According to this timetable, we
                    should be able to find Mr. Quick
                    upon the playing fields. He had a
                    theory lesson first thing and
                    then likely would have changed to
                    his sports wear for his next
                    lesson by now, poor fellow has to
                    then change back for a theory
                    lesson and then *again* for another
                    practical...what an irksome
                    arrangement

Holmes folds the timetable and places into his back pocket as
he opens up a gate leading on to the pitch.

                              HOLMES
                    Anyhow, I shall let you take the
                    lead with this one Watson as you
                    will be able to relate to him
                    better


                              WATSON
          How so Holmes?

                    **HOLMES**
          Remember what Miss Constance said
          he has gambling debts…you can
          sympathize

Watson seems a little offended and put out by this.

                    **WATSON**
          Oh come now Holmes that's a
          trifle unfair…that was more than
          one hundred or so years ago


                    **HOLMES**
mmm...


                    **WATSON**
          Can I have my cheque book back
          yet?


                    **HOLMES**
No


                    **WATSON**
          Fair enough, probably for the
          best…


Holmes and Watson continue to walk until they come to a tall
well-built tracksuit wearing man in his mid-twenties. He is
watching a group of children play football as he claps his
hands together shouting encouragement.


                    **MR.QUICK**
          That's it lads…pick it up pick it
          up…Oooh beautiful well done
          Smithy


                    **HOLMES**
          Mr. Quick?


                    **MR QUICK**
          Can I help you?

**HOLMES**

My name is Sherlock Holmes and
this is my friend and colleague
Dr.Watson


**WATSON**

We would like to ask you some
questions about the theft at the
Academy this morning


**MR QUICK**

Oh yeah Police right of
course…yeah ask away whatever I
can tell you to help

Watson and Holmes exchange a look of amusement.

**WATSON**

Err no we are not actually Police

Mr. Quick looks first at Holmes then to Watson slightly
puzzled.

**MR QUICK**

No? Oh so where are the Police?


**WATSON**

Miss Constance was of the view
she did not wish to involve
Police…hoping we would be able to
discover the thief without
causing embarrassment to the
Academy and presumably allow the
thief to simply resign reputation
intact…these are her wishes and
we are to honour them


**MR QUICK**

Private Investigators? Right…no
offence guys I am sure you are
good and all but I just thought
this was kind of serious you know
and would warrant Police
involvement…

                    WATSON
        You would rather the Police were
        involved?


                    MR QUICK
        Well…yeah whatever it takes to
        get the money back so the kids
        can go on the trip

Watson and Holmes exchange a suspicious glance.

                    WATSON
        Mr Quick…forgive me for being
        frank but we have been told that
        you have some outstanding
        payments looming on your head, is
        this correct?


                    MR QUICK
        Ah…So Miss Constance's tongue has
        been rolling…fair enough…yeah…I
        see what you are getting at but
        no, you are wrong


                    WATSON
        So you do not have any debts…

Mr. Quick rubs the back of his neck uneasy and shuffles his
feet slightly before relenting.

                    MR QUICK
        Ok I'll tell you…I admit when I
        was younger I was no angel, where
        I grew up there was never really
        anything for kids to do. I played
        a lot of football but they
        tarmacked over the park to make a
        supermarket…still carried it on
        round the streets but it was
        never the same, scoring a goal
        one minute between bundles of
        jumpers then leaping out of the
        way of a car the next


                    WATSON
        Oh dear…


                        119

**MR QUICK**

With no where to go and no money
to do it with I fell into the
wrong crowd and they got me into
gambling...little things at first,
slot machines, fiver on this
horse there, tenner on that game
there...but soon it turned to more
than just a flutter...black
jack...roulette...poker. I won a bit
and lost a lot,I was way over my
head in debts and out of my mind,
the only thing I had left that I
really still liked that didn't
cost me a penny was my football.
Kept that up through thick and
thin and *that* Mr Watson was my
life saver

**WATSON**

How so?

**MR QUICK**

Mr. Bruce Stock saw me play. He
is the founder of this academy...he
is a good man, a very good man,
he asked me right off there and
then if I ever thought of
teaching it...course I hadn't
"Whose this old duffer" I
thought. But he didn't give up
and carried on and well he told
me about his academy and how he
needed a Games Master for it

Mr. Quick looks to the Academy building with a far away look
in his eye.

**MR QUICK**

Wanted me to do it...said he saw
potential and what can I say...I
took the opportunity and ran with
it and well here I am two years
on...yeah I've still got some debts
to clear, but at least I am doing
some good for these kids and
earning the money for it legally
know what I mean?

                              HOLMES
                  Yes, I am familiar with the
                  concept of earning money under
                  legal circumstances


                             MR QUICK
                  So stealing from Mr. Stock after
                  all he did for me? Out of the
                  question, if these kids don't get
                  the opportunities to better
                  themselves and experience life
                  then they might not be so lucky
                  like it turned out for me…there
                  aren't many Mr. Stocks out there
                  you know

Mr. Quick returns his attention to the children playing
football.


                             MR QUICK
                  I so hope you get it back for us
                  gents, it ain't fair on the kids
                  otherwise…OY Fletcher…that's not
                  where javelins go is it? No don't
                  apologize to me apologize to
                  Robinson…sorry gents I had better
                  go, boys will be boys eh come see
                  if you need anything else.

Holmes tips his head to him as he sprints off onto the playing
field watched by Holmes and Watson.

                             WATSON
                  Well he seemed very nice didn't
                  he Holmes

Holmes glares after him.

                             HOLMES
                  Too nice…


                             WATSON
                  Oh for Goodness sake Holmes…I
                  expect if he had been rude you
                  would think him innocent…he was
                  reformed clearly!


                               121

                    **HOLMES**
          As was Mr. Braderick Theobald
          supposedly but just because
          someone is *nice* it does not
          absolve them from the blame of a
          crime…but neither does it condemn
          them I was merely stating he was
          very amiable. Still we shall need
          to speak to Miss Bliss before I
          formulate a definitive opinion on
          the matter

Holmes leans in close to Watson and in a pantomime stage
whisper utters.

                    **HOLMES**
          *Better get you're best whispering
          voice ready Watson*


                    **WATSON**
          I beg your pardon Holmes…why?


                    **HOLMES**
          *Because! It is off to Library
          land we go*

Watson blinks a few times then shakes his head baffled.

                    **WATSON**
          Pardon?


                    **HOLMES**
          *I said its off to the Library*


                    **WATSON**
          I can't hear what you are saying


                    **HOLMES**
          OH…just follow me…

Holmes throws hands in air in a resigned fed up manner and
begins stalking off.

                                        FADE OUT

## SCENE 8
## INT: HOLMES/WATSON LIVING ROOM

Miss Blake has finished her phone call now and crosses the living room to return to her seat.

>                    **MISS BLAKE**
>           Sorry about that…Oh Gawd Auntie
>           Pat couldn't believe I was going
>           to be in HELLO, won't she be so
>           surprised when she sees the next
>           issue

>                    **MADELINE**
>           Err…surprised…yes err but
>           speaking of family is that a
>           relative of yours in that photo
>           there?

Madeline points above the fireplace to the photograph of Irene Adler given to him by The King of Bohemia [SCAN].

Miss Blake squints at it then gets up taking it off the shelf to get a better look.

>                    **MISS BLAKE**
>           Oh that…no…this…this…is Mr.
>           Holmes Grandmother when she was
>           young…

Miss Blake hands the photo to Madeline.

>                    **MISS BLAKE**
>           Least I think it is…it's one of
>           the very few things he brought
>           when he moved in…and though he
>           has never actually *said* it is his
>           Grandma I assume so because its
>           old fashioned looking all black
>           and white and that and everyone
>           knows the world wasn't in colour
>           until the 1960's

>                    **BRADERICK**
>           WHAAAT…the world wasn't in colour
>           until the 1960s?

                    **MISS BLAKE**
          Well yeaaaah…they didn't invent
          it until then…I thought everyone
          knew that anyway we know it is
          true, I have seen the photos

Madeline raises eyebrow and rolls eyes.


                    **MADELINE**
          Right…yes if you say so…mmm…

Madeline turns it over and notes an inscription written on the
back, she frowns then copies this down into her own note pad
muttering the name as she does.


                    **MADELINE**
          …Irene Adler…


                                        FADE OUT


## SCENE 9
## INT: LIBRARY

Holmes and Watson enter from the far left of the school
Library and glance around taking in the environment. There is
a table nearby with a pale-skinned woman seated. She is in her
mid 20's dressed in a white short sleeve blouse and black
skirt reading silently.

                    **WATSON**
          I say Holmes…what a picturesque
          little library this is

Miss Bliss raises finger to mouth aggressively.

                    **MISS BLISS**
          SSSSHHH!!!


                    **WATSON**
          Oh but I only…

Miss Bliss points at Watson.

                    **MISS BLISS**
          That is two strikes! One more and
          I shall have to ask you to leave

Watson blinks a few times shaking his head not quite believing
her attitude before he turns to Holmes muttering irritated.

> **WATSON**
> Hmmph...it is like the Diogenes
> club all over again...

> **MISS BLISS**
> That is it! YOU please leave!

Holmes sniggers and nudges an astonished Watson.

> **HOLMES**
> Consider yourself fair warned
> dear fellow

Miss Bliss now points at Holmes.

> **MISS BLISS**
> YOU! First warning!

Holmes stands open-mouthed slightly taken aback by this as
Watson smirks back at him.

Holmes regains his composure as Miss Bliss returns to reading
then walks over throwing his calling card down on to the book
she is reading forcing her to look.

> **MISS BLISS**
> OH...Mr. Holmes! Yes the
> detective...yes...yes the theft oh
> dear, I mean um Rebecca did say
> you would be coming oh I am so
> sorry...I did not realize ...I...um

> **HOLMES**
> You seem...somewhat nervous Miss
> Bliss there really is no need to
> be now then for all I wa...

Miss Bliss interrupts.

> **MISS BLISS**
> I really do not know anything...I
> was not here till eight thirty
> this morning... normally its before
> but my bike had a slow puncture
> so I had to go very slowly...and
> the night before...the night before
> I was with my fiancé all evening
> he can tell you...SO I COULDN'T
> HAVE DONE IT...I COULDN'T HAVE!

Miss Bliss bursts into tears and lays head on table.

**WATSON**
Now Miss Bliss please calm
yourself Mr. Holmes did not say
you had...we just wanted to ask you
your account

Miss Bliss stops crying and looks up uncertain.

**MISS BLISS**
But you suspect me?

Holmes and Watson exchange suspicious glances.

**HOLMES**
Not necessarily...should we?

**MISS BLISS**
Well YES! I mean no...I mean ooh I
don't know but it is always the
quiet ones isn't it...and I'm the
quiet one...and its always the one
you least suspect AND IM likely
to be the least likely someone
would suspect...so there you MUST
assume its me BUT ITS NOT !!!!

Holmes goes to open mouth but is cut off.

**MISS BLISS**
Everything I have said is true
EVERYTHING please don't have me
arrested...I'll get a criminal
record and then I won't be able
to go to Australia if you do

Miss Bliss bursts into tears and lays head down buried into
her arms sobbing uncontrollably.

Holmes moves forward and awkwardly places hand on her shoulder
patting it to comfort her.

**HOLMES**
There...there Miss Bliss, if
everything you have said is true
then you have nothing to fear, as
I *will* find the answer...

Holmes takes hand off her and glances around.

                              HOLMES
                    NOW I must speak with Miss
                    Constance once more…

Holmes turns to leave but attention is drawn to a book upon
the table he picks it up looking puzzled until he reads the
title and lets out a short sharp laugh.


                              HOLMES
                    HAH…he actually went and got it
                    published unbelievable… actually
                    in the circumstances as the path
                    my life took perhaps he was not
                    quite as mad as I initially
                    thought…he took my advise on the
                    pen name too…still no time for
                    fairy tales…come along Watson

Holmes pushes the book into Watson's hands as he passes then
strides out.


                              WATSON
                    …The Time Machine…H.G Wells?


                            MISS BLISS
                    I hope you are not thinking of
                    getting that out…there's a six-
                    month loan ban on anyone who
                    disobeys the three-strike rule


                              WATSON
                    Uh…no sorry I was just…wait six
                    months? That is a tad harsh do
                    you not think!?…and hold…what am
                    I talking about I don't even go
                    to this school…

Watson glares at Miss Bliss as he places the book down
and she glares straight back at him.


                              HOLMES
                    WATSON!!! Come on!

Watson shakes his head at Miss Bliss and then walks away to
follow Holmes.

## SCENE 10
## INT: STAFF ROOM

Miss Constance is on the far right of the staff room, her coat clutched to her chest with one hand and the other being used to text on her phone.

Holmes and Watson approach from the left hand side.

> **HOLMES**
> Miss Constance?

Miss Constance jumps slightly in surprise before turning around.

> **MISS CONSTANCE**
> Ah Mr. Holmes have you found the cash? Which one was it? Miss Bliss am I right? It is always the quiet ones

> **HOLMES**
> She was perhaps a little over board in her defence yes…but there is one further test I would like to conduct to conclude this matter…can I request you Mr. Quick and Miss Bliss attend my house

> **MISS CONSTANCE**
> Right now?

> **HOLMES**
> The sooner the better if you could please yes…

Miss Constance seems slightly surprised by this but nods and goes to leave.

                         MISS CONSTANCE
                Very well I shall go get fetch
                them and meet you at the gates in
                ten minutes…do you mind switching
                off the lights on your way out?
                The switch is just there on the
                wall


                            HOLMES
                Of course Miss Constance

Miss Constance exits.

                            WATSON
                …Holmes will you really be able
                to get the money back? You know
                where it is?

Holmes turns and smiles smugly.

                            HOLMES
                I do…


                            WATSON
                But you're not going to tell me
                yet are you? Your going to leave
                me in the dark until the last
                possible minute aren't you?

Holmes frowns and pats Watson's shoulder as he passes to leave
the room.

                            HOLMES
                When have I ever done that
                Watson?


Holmes switches the light out plunging the room into complete
darkness.

                            WATSON
                HOLMES!!!!


SCENE 11
INT: HOLMES/WATSON LIVING ROOM

Miss Blake continues to blab away as Madeline continues to
scribe frantically.

                    MISS BLAKE
          So aside from Doctor
          Watson…another friend he often
          talks about is this other guy…err
          Les bit of a dim guy by the sound
          of it, Mr. Holmes has never
          introduced him to me either
          though…dunno why, maybe he's fat?
          Anyway Mr. Trade…that is it yeah
          Les Trade!


                    MADELINE
          Friend…Les…Trade uhhuh ok good
          good and…oh excuse me

She roots in her bag for her phone that is beginning to buzz
and vibrate and after reading the message on screen her eyes
widen and she becomes visibly panicked.

                    MADELINE
          Christine…sweetie we are going to
          have to cut this short I'm afraid


                    MISS BLAKE
          Awww but you didn't get to hear
          about the time my Auntie Pat and
          I went shoe shopping in
          Brighton…THAT was a scream, I
          don't think the jelly fish
          thought so but then I don't think
          jelly fish think really can they?

Madeline begins packing up her bag in a hurry rolls her eyes
and mutters.

                    MADELINE
          Then it must have been in good
          company then clearly…


                    MISS BLAKE
     Huh?

Madeline stands up smiles and begins to usher a bewildered
Braderick up from the sofa.

                            MADELINE
                    Nothing sweetie…well its too bad
                    so sad but we really must dash…I
                    have err…just got wind that a
                    certain Hollywood star has just
                    had a bad hair cut…*with*
                    highlights


                            MISS BLAKE
                    OMIGOD Realeee?? Quick you better
                    go, I don't want to miss out on
                    that in the next issue hurry
                    hurry go!!!

Miss Blake excitedly pushes them both from behind out of the
living room.


                            MADELINE
                    Thank you for the interview
                    Christine…and all you told
                    us…very useful


                            MISS BLAKE
                    OH wait you didn't get any
                    photos!

Braderick pulls out his phone and turns it to the side
attempting to start taking photos with it only to be pulled
away by Madeline much to Miss Blake's confusion.

                            MISS BLAKE
                    …OK BYE…looking forward to the
                    issue…give my love to Brangelina
                    next time you see them…

The door slams and they exit house.

                                              FADE OUT



SCENE 12
EXT: STREET


Madeline and Braderick scurry down the pathway from the house.

                            BRADERICK
                    Did we get enough?

                    **MADELINE**
          A damn lot more than we knew
          before about him, I knew she
          would fall for it...dippy bird


                    **BRADERICK**
          I wish I had got a few more
          photos though...you know a few
          medium shots...some profiles would
          have been nice...she has a good
          bone structure you know


                    **MADELINE**
          Huh? Idiot...were not REALLY making
          an article on her


                    **BRADERICK**
          Oh...I knew that


                    **MADELINE**
          Tut...come on before Mr. Holmes and
          Dr Watson come back and spot us
          both here

They begin walking off down the street quickly.

                    **BRADERICK**
          So who's this celebrity with the
          bad hair cut?


                    **MADELINE**
          Ooooh...shut up!!!

                                        FADE OUT

## SCENE 13
### INT: HOLMES/WATSON LIVING ROOM

Open to Miss Bliss upon the Sofa, Miss Constance and Watson standing on the far left nearest to French windows.

Mr. Quick and Holmes are in the centre of room.

Holmes surveys his audience and once convinced he has their complete attention addresses them.

> **HOLMES**
> Thank you all for coming so quickly...I shall not delay you any further and come straight to the point

> **MR QUICK**
> So you have found the money? The kids can go on the trip?

> **HOLMES**
> All in good time Mr. Quick...all in good time...I...oh

Holmes pauses and frowns at Mr. Quick

> **HOLMES**
> Mr. Quick...while it is not normally within my nature to make any fashion statements of sorts or dispense advise I feel I really must say that baggy sports wear really does you no favours

> **MR QUICK**
> Eh?

Holmes begins tugging at Mr. Quicks shell suit.

> **HOLMES**
> What I mean is...look it is frankly slovenly and you are undoubtedly a physically fit man but the way the cloth bulges out like this, why it makes you look positively round in the middle...not a good look for a Physical Education teacher

Mr. Quick looks baffled by this.

                    MR QUICK
            Well...eh...hang on a minute


                    WATSON
            Holmes what are you doing?

Holmes begins smoothing and straightening out Mr. Quicks
clothing much to his discomfort and confusion.

                    HOLMES
            Here let me straighten this out
            for you...see lets smooth that down
            here...and oh I know what would
            also help perhaps it would look
            better if we removed...THIS

Holmes pulls out a bulky envelope from one of the jacket
pockets and throws it to Watson who promptly peers inside.


                    WATSON
            Good Lord...there must be hundreds
            of pounds here

Mr Quick looks gob smacked as Miss Bliss turns to him in
anger.

                    MISS BLISS
            Tristan! How could you


                    MR QUICK
            Wait woah woah no I have never
            seen that before in MY LIFE...no
            way would I do it...no way at all


                    MISS CONSTANCE
            After all we did for you and
            after all Mr. Stock did

Mr. Quick holds his hands up defensively before turning to
Holmes and jabbing his finger aggressively towards him.

                    MR QUICK
            NO, I didn't do anything...this is
            a mistake...YOUR making a mistake

                              HOLMES
                    Perhaps Watson it would do Mr.
                    Quick some good to step outside
                    and cool down in the garden for a
                    bit…would you escort him please…

Watson glances out the windows concerned.

                              WATSON
                    But Holmes…it's starting to rain?


                              HOLMES
                    IS it…oh well all the more reason
                    to then…in that case EVERYONE
                    outside

Everyone apart from Holmes exchange bewildered expressions.

                          MISS CONSTANCE
                    Excuse me?

Holmes slides open the door to the French window where outside
it is lashing down with rain.

                              HOLMES
                    You heard me…EVERYONE
                    outside…come on look lively you
                    should be pleased Miss Constance
                    we have recovered the money I
                    just think certain frayed tempers
                    could do with cooling…

The teachers and Watson reluctantly trudge past Holmes into
the pouring rain.

                                              FADE OUT




SCENE 14
EXT:OUTSIDE HOLMES HOUSE

Miss Blake is walking up the pathway from the house just about
to pull up her umbrella when a suddenly a man wearing a red
hooded rain coat springs up from behind a bush giving Miss
Blake a jolt.

                           MISS BLAKE
                    OH…hello Mr.Phillimore… I didn't
                    see you there sorry

                    **MR PHILLIMORE**
Hello Miss Blake that is quite
all right…I am most unnoticeable

He pauses and looks up alarmed at the darkened sky holding his
hand out expectantly.

                    **MR PHILLIMORE**
Oh dear it does rather look like
rain doesn't it

Miss Blake glances upwards and nods.

                    **MISS BLAKE**
Err yes yes I guess it does

                    **MR PHILLIMORE**
I am just going to go back into
my house now…to fetch an umbrella

                    **MISS BLAKE**
…Ok…

                    **MR PHILLIMORE**
…I expect I will see you later

                    **MISS BLAKE**
Err yes…yes I expect you will
wont you…

                    **MR PHILLIMORE**
That is of course is if once I go
into my house to get my
umbrella…I *am never seen again*…in
which case then I wont see you
later…

                    **MISS BLAKE**
Er…no you wouldn't would you…

                    **MR PHILLIMORE**
Toodlepip…

He slinks off behind a bush and promptly out of sight leaving
a slightly dazed Miss Blake shaking her head slightly baffled
before turning placing her umbrella up and walking down the
road as the rain begins to pick up faster and faster.

                                           FADE OUT


**SCENE 15**
**EXT: GARDEN**

Holmes and Watson and the teachers stand shivering in a line
as the rain continues to beat down.


Holmes is remarkably cheerful, everyone else looks cold and
miserable.

                         **MR QUICK**
                I didn't do it...I didn't

Miss Constance clutches the coat she is carrying closer to her
chest and whispers to Miss Bliss irritated.

                       **MISS CONSTANCE**
                I know his methods are eccentric
                but this is downright stupid...I am
                going to get soaked



                         **WATSON**
                Holmes how much longer are we
                going to be out here? Everyone is
                going to catch a frightful cold!



                         **MR QUICK**
                ...I didn't do it...please someone
                listen to me I wouldn't! Why
                won't anyone believe me?



                         **HOLMES**
                Mr. Quick...I do believe you and in
                fact not once have I actually
                *said* that you were the thief now
                have I?

Everyone looks at Holmes shocked.


                           137

                    **WATSON/MISS BLISS**
          What?


                      **MR QUICK**
          I...I...oh...err no you didn't I just
          assumed that


                       **HOLMES**
          Well that's what you get for
          assuming without thinking

Holmes glances at the other two teachers then claps his hands.

                       **HOLMES**
          NOW I think I have seen enough
          EVERYONE BACK INSIDE


Miss Constance shakes her head wearily as they all turn and
walk back towards the house.

                                        FADE OUT


**SCENE 16**
**INT: HOLMES/WATSON LIVING ROOM**


Miss Bliss and Miss Constance enter the living room first and
walk to the far end of the room nearest the French windows
once again. Miss Bliss shakes her head confused.


                     **MISS BLISS**
          I don't understand?


                    **MISS CONSTANCE**
          Neither do I


                     **MISS BLISS**
          But what is going on?

Miss Constance shrugs.

                    **MISS CONSTANCE**
          Search me


                         138

Holmes Watson and Mr. Quick enter at this point with Holmes
leading first.

                    HOLMES
          Thank you for the permission to
          go ahead and do so Miss Constance
          as this was actually my next move


                    MISS CONSTANCE
          Wait…what???

Holmes tugs at the coat she was clutching tightly to her chest
causing it to drop to the floor, as he does so a large
envelope with a rectangular lump drops out with it.

Holmes picks it up and rips it open at the top before flinging
over his shoulder to Watson who peers inside.

                    WATSON
          Good Lord…there must be THOUSANDS
          in this one…


                    HOLMES
          Well yes Watson a school trip to
          Switzerland is a pricey
          affair…though the full cost is of
          course if we total up the other
          envelope too

Miss Constance backs away slightly as Miss Bliss and Mr Quick
stare at her in horror.

                    MISS CONSTANCE
          I…I…no there's been a mistake…


                    HOLMES
          Yes there has…thankfully for Mr.
          Quick and Miss Bliss…all of them
          made by you


                    MR QUICK
          Wait am I hearing this right…SHE
          did it?


                    MISS BLISS
          How could you Rebecca?

## MISS CONSTANCE

I...I...umm...I


## HOLMES

Am wondering how I knew? Shall we
start with your degree in the
staff room

CUT TO
FLASHBACK


SCENE 5
INT:STAFF ROOM

Holmes picks up and examines Miss Constance's Certificate


### *HOLMES*

*Look at this Watson a 2.1 in the
field of Theatre
Studies...admirable Miss
Constance...You were not then moved
to follow a life on stage?*

FADE OUT
RETURN TO
SCENE


## HOLMES

Notably it was in Drama,
something you have utilized very
well indeed to portray sincerity
and a false impression of
concern. If it weren't for the
other factors I would not have
seen through it and be pointing
it out now

                    **MR QUICK**
But what are the other
factors…how did the money get on
me?


                    **HOLMES**
Getting to it Mr. Quick… Miss
Constance you gave me a timetable
of Mr. Quicks lessons, I recall I
noted to Watson how tiresome it
was for him to change back and
forth between suit and track
wear.

                                        CUT TO
                                        FLASHBACK


SCENE 8
EXT: FOOTBALL FIELD


                    HOLMES
According to this time table we
should be able to find Mr. Quick
upon the playing fields…he had a
theory lesson first thing and
then likely would have changed to
his sports wear for his next
lesson by now…poor fellow has to
then change back for a theory
lesson and then AGAIN for another
practical…what an irksome
arrangement…

                                        FADE OUT
                                        RETURN TO
                                        SCENE


                    **WATSON**
So…the only other person to truly
know when he would be in the
field and when he was teaching in
class…would have been Miss
Constance therefore his sports
wear would have been easy to
access and slip the money in
during this time

141

                    **HOLMES**
Precisely...the idea being she *knew*
I would spot it and he would get
the blame and all it would cost
was the planting of an extract of
the total money she herself had
stolen.


                **MISS CONSTANCE**
I...err...um


                    **HOLMES**
But the clue that has been most
prominent time and time again
since I met you Miss Constance is
that coat

Holmes gestures to the black coat Miss Constance is still
clutching close to her waist.

                  **MR QUICK**
The coat?


                    **HOLMES**
When you first came to me
following the so called theft...you
recall I noted despite the rain
you had not put on your coat


                                            CUT TO
                                            FLASHBACK



SCENE 2
INT: HOLMES/WATSON LIVING ROOM




                  HOLMES
Please sit and explain the panic
that has caused you to act with
such haste you were unable to
even find time to actually put on
your coat before you fled from
Your headmistress post at the
highly respectable Bruce Stock
academy

                    142

### HOLMES

I put it down to being in a rush
but then again when we left in
the rain, you asked to borrow an
umbrella…odd…again you didn't
want to use your coat

### MISS CONSTANCE

I…can explain…

Holmes ignores her and carries on.

### HOLMES

In the staff room again you kept
your coat closely guarded to
you…which got me thinking…why
didn't you ever hang it up?

### MISS CONSTANCE

There has been some horrible mix
up…

### HOLMES

Lastly just now when I had us all
stand in the rain again despite
your protesting. You did not wear
your coat…this was the final
straw upon the camels back for me
to confirm what I thought

Watson ponders this briefly then nods.

### WATSON

…If she ever actually wore the
coat…the hidden package would
have stuck out like a sore thumb
like it did with Mr. Quick…and no
one would suspect to check the
very woman who called it in in
the first place…so it would have
remained safe bundled there

                              HOLMES
          Precisely

Miss Constance shakes head and snarls.

                         MISS CONSTANCE
          Oh you...you...snide smarmy arrogant
          busy body...you think your SOOO
          smart...you and...Dr...Bumble Brush
          face here


                              WATSON
          Well now really! Bumble Brush!
          Well this is just too much

Holmes begins to snigger and can hardly contain his laughter.

                              HOLMES
          Bumble Brush Face...ahhah um

Watson looks grave and sincere and obviously does not see the
funny side causing Holmes to stop and readdress his anger
towards Miss Constance.

                              HOLMES
          Madam...please refrain from
          insulting my friend...despite your
          name-calling I shall remain the
          gentleman in this situation and
          NOT that you deserve it I will
          honour our agreement of the
          Police not being involved


                            MR QUICK
          What? But I can't work with her
          not after this...she's insane! Look
          what she did


                              HOLMES
          And you wont have too...because in
          return she will resign from her
          post with immediate effect...and
          recommend you Mr. Quick as her
          replacement...you have good rapport
          with Mr. Stock I am sure he would
          agree...understood Miss Constance?

                        **MISS CONSTANCE**
                WHAT! I…yes completely, I…I will
                go clear out my office right away

She saunters past the disapproving glares of Miss Bliss
bumping past Watson's elbow before she stops and hesitantly
turns.

                        **MISS CONSTANCE**
                Miss Bliss…Mr Quick…I just want
                you to know…there are no hard
                feelings, it was never personal…I
                just wanted the
                money…lots…and…lots…of money…

She smirks before swiftly turns on her heels holding her head
up high saunters out of the room.

                        *SFX:*
                        *DOOR SLAM*

Watson raises his eyebrow and rests tongue against his cheek.

                        **WATSON**
                …Uh…huh…


                        **HOLMES**
                …yes…well…what a completely
                unredeemable woman that was

Mr. Quick crosses the room and shakes Holmes and Watson's
hands.

                        **MR QUICK**
                Mr Holmes…Dr Watson…what can I
                say but thank you…you two saved
                my life…my career…the kids…I
                don't know what Id have done if
                she had got away with it, if any
                lesser detective had been on the
                job I would have been done for

Holmes smiles at Watson.

                        **HOLMES**
                Well we do but try

                    MR QUICK
          If Mr. Stock approves me being
          the head...well I want you two to
          know...any kids you ever have I
          would see to it they could get
          free placements at the Stock
          Academy

Holmes doubles over and bursts out laughing much to Mr. Quicks
bafflement.

                    HOLMES
          HAH...Ah haah

Holmes regains composure and brushes tear from eye.

                    HOLMES
          Sorry...quite well thank you Mr.
          Quick that is an exceptionally
          kind offer, but one more likely
          to be of use to Watson one
          day...than myself...BUT there is
          perhaps something you can for me
          Miss Bliss

                  MISS BLISS
          Of course anything

Holmes places his hand on Watson's shoulder.

                    HOLMES
          If you could be so good as to
          lift the library ban upon my dear
          friend...it was really most of our
          character of him to be so
          disruptive like that

                    WATSON
          Wait...pardon?

Holmes turns to Miss Bliss pulling a face of complete
sincerity and sorrow.

                    HOLMES
          He has learnt his lesson I am
          sure and would be as quiet as a
          church mouse in future...would you
          not Watson?

Watson raises his eyebrows.

                    **MISS BLISS**
          Of course Mr. Holmes he is
          welcome to visit any time he
          likes…you both are


Holmes smiles cheekily at Watson and claps him on the shoulder
again.

                    **HOLMES**
          There you are Watson…unlimited
          access to the children's library
          once more…you can finally get
          those Twilight books Miss Blake
          keeps harping on about, they
          sound so appallingly written and
          absurd…like your writing…your
          sure to enjoy them

Watson grits his teeth and nods grim faced.

                    **WATSON**
          …thank you Holmes you are too
          kind…

                                        FADE TO
                                        BLACK


**FINAL SCENE**
**INT: MADELINES DUNGEON**

Madeline is busy going over her notepad at the dungeon table
as Braderick stands by her side glancing around puzzled.

                    **BRADERICK**
          Why do you have a dungeon in your
          house by the way?



                    **MADELINE**
          What…I don't know…

Madeline motions with her hand.

                    **MADELINE**
          It was just here…I inherited this
          from my Daddy and its been in the
          family for like over a hundred
          years…someone at some time
          obviously needed it and anyway,
          it is more villainous than doing
          all this in the living room

                    147

**BRADERICK**

> I'd quite like it if we operated
> from the living room…it would
> be…homely

Madeline fixes him with a steely glare and goes to open her
mouth only for her phone to start vibrating and ringing
causing her to forget about him as she picks it up

**WOMAN V/O**

> …Well I hope you are happy

Madeline grins and picks up her notebook.

**MADELINE**

> Exceptionally…the dippy
> housekeeper didn't shut up…
> She has given me a lot to work
> with…oh thanks for the warning
> they were on their way back by
> the way…everything worked
> perfectly

CUT TO

EXT: GROUNDS OF ACADEMY

Miss Constance hurries away from the academy clutching phone
to ear and with box of her cleared out possessions in the
other arm. She is clearly distressed and distraught.

**MISS CONSTANCE**

> NO it did bloody not…HE figured
> it out and that wasn't part of
> the plan…He forced me into
> resigning, I'm lucky I didn't get
> jailed! What am I supposed to do
> now…that was a bloody well paid
> job

CUT TO

148

INT: DUNGEON

> **MADELINE**
> Look don't worry about it…once
> Sherlock Holmes is out of the way
> there will be nothing to stop us
> amassing vast fortunes beyond our
> wildest dreams, lets face it
> looking after snot nosed kids was
> never your true calling
> anyway…trust me you wont regret
> the day you
> joined…The…Red…Headed…League

                                            CUT TO


EXT: GROUNDS OF ACADEMY

> **MISS CONSTANCE**
> …hmm true…now its official…at
> least I won't have to keep dying
> my hair any more

She balances phone between her ear and shoulder then plucks
out a box of brown hair dye from her box and tosses it over
her shoulder onto the ground behind her
before hurrying on.

> **MISS CONSTANCE**
> So…what happens now?

                                            CUT TO


INT: DUNGEON

Madeline stretches her hand out and examines her fingernails
coy before answering confidently.

> **MADELINE**
> We find out who Mr. Holmes *really*
> is…

                                            CUT TO

EXT: GROUNDS OF ACADEMY

Rebecca turns around as a clash of thunder booms out and the rain begins to fall even harder down as she surveys the darkening sky line.

                                                    CUT TO


INT: DUNGEON

Madeline places her phone down in front of her then leans back smiling to herself before burying her head back into the notebook.

Braderick is still glancing around until he suddenly his face is struck with a look of joy and revelation.


                        BRADERICK
            Curtains!

Madeline glances it him and shakes head confused.

                        MADELINE
            What?


                        BRADERICK
            …Curtains…that's what would look
            good down here…Curtains…and maybe
            a lampsha…


                        MADELINE
            OH SHUT UP

Braderick looks crest fallen and returns to looking down at the floor twiddling his hair nervously as Madeline scowls once more before returning to her reading.

                                                    FADE OUT




                        END

NO PLACE LIKE HOLMES
SERIES 3 EPISODE 3
"DIALYSIS MURDER"

ORIGINAL AIRING MARCH 30TH-APRIL 20TH 2013 (4 PARTS)

CAST

SHERLOCK HOLMES.................................................ROSS K FOAD
DR JOHN H.WATSON...........................................MIKE ARCHER
MISS CHRISTINE BLAKE.............................TAMZIN DUNSTONE
MISS TERESA FAIRWEATHER......................SAL BOLTON
MR HERBERT REEVES.........................................JOHN TSOPANIS
DANIEL "MOONSHINE" DIGWEED..............JOE SANDZ
RANGER BILL MCCREATH.............................BRETT UNDERWOOD
DOCTOR PROCTOR....................................................GENE FOAD
MADELINE CHAMBERS.........................................KELSEY WILLIAMS
REBECCA CONSTANCE.........................................ANGELA HOLMES

<u>**Scene 1**</u>
<u>**INT: HOLMES/WATSON LIVING ROOM**</u>


Open to find MISS BLAKE and WATSON side by side on the sofa,
Miss Blake is reading "HELLO" whilst Watson has a newspaper
open and appears to be reading an article, it is obviously
causing him great amusement and he chuckles quietly to himself
shaking his head in disbelief.


                          **WATSON**
             What rot and nonsense look at
             this Miss Blake…

Miss Blake peers over interested at first then confused.

                        **MISS BLAKE**
             What's that…hey where are all the
             pictures in your magazine? Its
             all long words and stuff…

Watson looks up frowning slightly but without looking to her
replies deadpan slowly.

                          **WATSON**
             Yes…worldly news tends to be…

Miss Blake squints eyes deep in thought processing this before
slowly nodding as if she has now managed to figure it out and
flicks through her own magazine.

                        **MISS BLAKE**
             Ahh right right…news…yeah there's
             a page of that somewhere in here
             sometimes…AH…see…Brad Pitt caught
             leaving salon…new hairstyle!!!

She taps the page proudly and turns to Watson elated as if
expecting him to be equally excited before turning her
attention back to the page looking slightly disappointed.

                        **MISS BLAKE**
             Mmm I wonder if this was the
             article Candy had to rush off and
             write…still can't find the one
             about me yet though…


Watson raises an eyebrow but carries on regardless.

                    **WATSON**
          Err yes but now listen to
          this…its completely absurd but
          animal rights campaigner and
          President of "The Parsnip Defence
          League…" Mr Daniel Moonshine
          Digweed…

He looks up and frowns shaking his head muttering to himself.

                    **WATSON**
          That can not be his real name
          surely?…Whom was jailed in 2010
          following a violent assault with
          a pitchfork upon a Huntington lab
          technician Mr. Gerald Travers of
          Wilmer Way SW10 because of
          rumours over the unregulated
          animal testing methods the
          company used…

Miss Blake frowns and then looks away from her attention being
fixed on Watson to biting her lip as if concentrating hard
murmuring to herself.

                    **MISS BLAKE**
          Tut…animal testing…I've never
          understood why scientists do that

                    **WATSON**
          How so? Do you mean morally how
          do they do it?

                    **MISS BLAKE**
          No I mean…what's the point…like
          take a rabbit right…what's the
          point of giving it the latest
          Rimmel Eye liner or something…it
          cant tell you whether it likes
          it…it wont even know whether the
          style is in fashion or not! See
          that is not good market research…

                    **WATSON**
          mmm…that's not quite why they do
          it Miss Blake…

                    153

                          **MISS BLAKE**
        Oh...



                          **WATSON**
        Anyhow, as I was saying,
        Moonshine...was allowed out on day
        release yesterday unsupervised in
        light of his pending release from
        being held at her majesties
        pleasure...when lo and behold... the
        very laboratory technician he
        clearly begrudged...winds up being
        murdered in his own home by means
        of a pitchfork...



                          **MISS BLAKE**
        NO!!!


Watson expression turns more grim as he shakes his head even
taking a breath before continuing.

                          **WATSON**
        Yes...but if that's not coincidental
        enough...well the police found blood
        at the scene, which matches...which
        matches none other than this Mr...Moon
        Beam...Digweed chap



                          **MISS BLAKE**
        Wow...

Watson frowns again as he examines the paper.

                              WATSON
              And this is the most preposterous
              thing though...but he proclaims
              complete and utter innocence and
              that he went nowhere near the
              technicians home...and he goes as
              far as to say the fresh cut upon
              his own hand that they have found
              is completely unrelated to his
              blood being found in the
              technician's home...but can't say
              where he did get it from nor
              account for his whereabouts for
              the day in question...

Miss Blake shakes head and leans back slightly on sofa.

                            MISS BLAKE
              Who does he expect will believe
              that then? Gawd even I can figure
              that one out...only one thing for
              it then...book him Dano ay...


                              WATSON
              Pardon? Who is Dano?

Miss Blake laughs and slaps him lightly on the arm
affectionately.

                            MISS BLAKE
              God John you are so funny
              sometimes "Whose Dano?"

Watson looks at her baffled and returns to looking at his
paper none the wiser as Miss Blake returns to looking at her
magazine.


                            MISS BLAKE
              Well one thing is for certain
              anyway...THAT is one case Mr Holmes
              definitely won't be needed to be
              consulted on...

                                             CUT TO

**INT:PRISON ROOM**

HOLMES sits opposite a long haired scruffy blonde man in a
prison uniform wringing his hands nervously frequently
glancing up and down, eye twitching clearly very worried.

Holmes is dressed in a prison guard uniform *(Dark blue thick
sweater, peaked cap, utility belt, baton, keys)* his hands are
steeped together as he stares intently across the table from
the prisoner.

> **HOLMES**
> Well Mr Digweed…I have listened
> to what you have to say and…I
> would very much like to help
> you…and I believe that I can

FADE OUT

**SCENE 2**
**INT: PRISON ROOM**

Holmes sits opposite Digweed still; the room is barren save
the table and two chairs. Digweed nods nervously eyes
repeatedly roaming the room casting fleeting glances to
Holmes.

> **DIGWEED**
> …w…w…wait s…so you believe me?
> That I didn't kill the man

> **HOLMES**
> I believe it is possible you did
> not…

> **DIGWEED**
> …wow…

> **HOLMES**
> You proclaim innocence yet seem
> surprised when I say I have not
> assumed you guilty Mr. Digweed…

156

Digweed eyes him up and down suspiciously.

> **DIGWEED**
> I don't know why you would want
> to help me

> **HOLMES**
> First off Mr Digweed…

> **DIGWEED**
> Call me Moonshine

Holmes scowls and leans forward annoyed.

> **HOLMES** [CONT]
> I will do no such thing…now pray
> take heart Mr Digweed for first
> off your fiancé clearly believes
> you did not commit such a crime.

> **DIGWEED**
> My Fiancé? Teresa sent you?

> **HOLMES**
> Yes I do apologize my
> introduction was scant and hasty
> for I have very little time as
> you may have gathered I should be
> here no more than Aardvark should
> be found in the E's

                                        CUT TO
                                        FLASH BACK

**SCENE 2B**
**INT: HOLMES LIVING ROOM**

A woman in her late 20's stands wringing her hands on a tissue
clearly very upset and distraught.

Upon the sofa sits a short timid speckled man in glasses and
gardening gloves hands on knees watching the woman intently.

Holmes stands opposite one arm folded the other hand placed on
his chin as he is in deep in thought over what he is being
told.

                    **TERESA**
          He wouldn't do it Mr Holmes…he
          couldn't…murder…it is not in his
          nature…I'm not saying Mr. Travers
          did not deserve it mind…foul
          horrible man…the experiments he
          was responsible for were
          inhumane…so he DID deserve it
          …but Daniel had nothing to do
          with it!



                    **HOLMES**
          Well…on the contrary given his
          previous conviction and reason
          for being in prison…I am sorry to
          inform you it may very well
          actually be in his nature…

TERESA shakes her head pulls out her wallet and begins taking
out credit card sized membership cards and handing them to
Holmes as she pulls each one out.

                    **TERESA**
          No no your wrong it cant be…I can
          prove it…look at these clubs and
          movements he is part of…not only
          is he the proud leader of the
          parsnip defence league…but also
          look he is a supporter of *Pulses
          For The Poor*. That's our
          campaign for a policy of free
          lentils for those in financial
          constraint, *Badger Mating Not
          Bating*, *Give Cows Choices and
          Voices* …don't you think its
          disgusting in this day and age
          that just because someone is a
          bovine they are denied the right
          to vote

Holmes frowns unsure if she is being serious but the look on
her face is one of complete conviction and seriousness.

                    **HOLMES**
          Err…appallingly so…yes…I am sure
          the Suffragettes would have got
          round to addressing it if they
          had had the time…

                    **TERESA**
          I quite agree…but my point is
          look at all the good he was
          trying to do before he was put
          away…what kind of man would do
          all of this and then go and
          murder

The man on the sofa nervously sticks his hand up and pipes
out.

                    **HERBERT**
          Might I add…don't forgot Teresa
          but he is also an organ donor,
          agreed to do a kidney
          transplant…didn't even know the
          man…just signed up to do it as
          and when it was needed. And *that*
          Mr. Holmes speaks volumes of his
          character…

HERBERT pauses and removes a tissue from pocket wiping his
nose before carrying on.

                    **HERBERT**
          When I heard they accused him of
          murder…why it was such a shock I
          actually had a nose bleed

Teresa shakes head and sighs folding arms.

                    **TERESA**
          …Herbert you ALWAYS have nose
          bleeds…

                    **HERBERT**
          Well I haven't always though have
          I…err…yes but even so…

                    **TERESA**
          Quite…see Mr. Holmes, Daniel has
          to be on permanent dialysis now
          because of giving up a kidney…his
          remaining one as it turns out is
          not very good…he didn't even know
          who it went to…yes he made a poor
          judgement to attack the
          technician all those years ago
          but would a man like this murder?

Holmes frowns and looks around and realises its coming from
Herbert who is patting at his jacket.

                    **HERBERT**
          So terribly sorry…do please,
          carry on

Holmes mouth twitches and he rubs his chin in thought thinking
it through before looking up to face Teresa.

                    **HOLMES**
          Aside from the one assault he
          does sound an unlikely candidate
          for murder, I also question why
          so close to his release date he
          would risk doing this…


                    **TEREASA**
          So you can help? You'll be able
          to clear him of this


                    **HOLMES**
          Well…not if he actually committed
          it no… there are still some very
          key questions that need
          answering, how his blood came to
          be found by the deceased for a
          start


                    **TERESA**
          There must be an
          explanation…there must be…please
          say you will look into it…

Holmes folds his arm and stares at the ground for a few
seconds before glancing at Herbert and then finally onto
Teresa.

                    **HOLMES**
          I will indeed look into it but I
          cannot promise you will like what
          I find…

                                        CUT TO

## SCENE 2C
## INT: PRISON ROOM

Holmes looks around warily to ensure nobody is listening in before he continues.

> **HOLMES**
> Now getting in to see you was not
> easy…your visiting rights have
> been curtailed…hence this
> disguise…but I am not above
> suspicion so I am going to need
> your assistance in answering some
> questions as quickly as
> possible…because there are some
> very curious incidents that
> occurred in that night-time. For
> a start, why can you not say what
> you were doing that night?

Digweed shifts his attention from Holmes to his feet and rubs the back of his neck.

> **DIGWEED**
> Oh yeah well…see the reason I
> can't tell is because …well I
> might get in trouble because
> well…all right…I'll tell you…on
> my day release I met up with
> Herbie Reevey

> **HOLMES**
> That is your friend…Mr Herbert
> Reeves?

> **DIGWEED**
> Yeah Herbie, he might seem a
> square but under the glasses…he's
> a dude

                              HOLMES
          A dude you say?...mmm interesting...I
          am not familiar with that
          occupation...I had him down as
          being a gardener

Digweed suddenly starts sniffing and holds his fist up to his
nose.

                             DIGWEED
          Oh yeah that too...but...err sorry Mr
          Holmes I couldn't score a tissue
          off you could I?

                              HOLMES
          Err yes, I believe I have a spare
          handkerchief...

Holmes frowns then pats his pockets eventually extracting one
and handing it over to Digweed who takes it and stuffs it
against his nose.

                             DIGWEED
          Ah...that's better...sorry man...

He hands it back to Holmes who looks slightly disgusted at it
and gingerly takes it in one finger before wrapping in another
tissue and pocketing it.

                         DIGWEED [CONT]
          ...look ive been in here along
          time...its kinda the dull sound of
          drums so I thought I gotta use
          this freedom wisely...so yeah we
          did some doobie...

                              HOLMES
          ...you did some... "doobie"?

Digweed looks shocked and looks around worried moving his
finger to his lips.

                             DIGWEED
          SSHH not so loud man...if *the man*
          hears they'll know...and that's an
          automatic extension to my
          sentence if they knew...

                    **HOLMES**
           ...AHH...narcotics...yes...I am
           familiar......wait so am I correct in
           thinking you could not tell them
           why you couldn't remember  your
           movements...because you feared you
           would be in trouble for your drug
           use?


                    **DIGWEED**
           Right


                    **HOLMES**
           Mr.Digweed... might I remind you
           that you are currently under
           suspicion of murder...

Digweed sighs and leans back shaking his head.

                    **DIGWEED**
           I know...it's a drag isn't it?
           But yeah...I remember...there were
           stairs...and a floor...and there was
           some degree of drug hazed
           falling...in between...

Holmes snaps his fingers excited and darts forward grabbing
Digweed's hand turning it over and examining the injury.

                    **HOLMES**
           Which explains the cut upon your
           hand...it's not a struggle wound!
           It is a...drug hazed fallen wound.
           This is a start...but please be
           very frank with me Mr. Digweed
           have you any idea then how blood
           they have matched to you was
           found to be at the scene?


                    **DIGWEED**
           Look...I'm sorry I can't remember
           all that much but like all I did
           was chill out...and all I know Mr.
           Holmes is I swear swear SWEAR to
           you I was no where near Gillette
           Grove

Holmes eyes light up again and he leans forward.

                              **HOLMES**
                   Where did you just say you where
                   nowhere near…

                              **DIGWEED**
                   Gillette Grove…it's where the guy
                   lived…number 18 I remember that
                   much from when I looked him up
                   and…

Holmes leaps up excited and begins pacing the cell.

                              **HOLMES**
                   THIS…is interesting…for the
                   newspaper puts the murder taking
                   place at Travers home address in
                   Wilmer Way…so I…err what's that
                   noise?


                              *SFX:*
                   *BEEP BEEP BEEP*

Holmes looks around puzzled as does Digweed until suddenly
Digweed remembers its him and reaches into his pocket pulling
out a small white electric device.



                              **DIGWEED**
                   OH its time for my dialysis
                   appointment…this keeps track of
                   them you see…monitors the
                   levels…I donated one of my
                   kidneys and its not a very good
                   one left so yeah I have to have
                   this…say are you the guard that's
                   taking me to the hospital wing
                   today?

Holmes looks about puzzled left to right then slowly shakes
his head.

                              **HOLMES**
                   …No I'm not a real guard…remember

Digweed nods but clearly is none the wiser.

                              **DIGWEED**
                   Right…right…sooo…then…you…are…


                                 164

                              HOLMES
                 Sigh...I am Sherlock Holmes...I'm
                 here to find the truth...

Digweed holds his fingers out in a peace sign.

                              DIGWEED
                 OH Radical!

Holmes frowns and gets off seat adjusting cap and mutters as
he is leaving.

                              HOLMES
                 Stay off the "Doobie" will
                 you...for both our sakes...?


                                                   FADE OUT


SCENE 3
INT: Holmes Living room

Open to find Miss Blake on sofa looking left and right to
arguing Holmes and Watson trying to follow the flow of the
thread but only being rather baffled.

H+W stand in front of fireplace facing one another as Watson
looks exasperated holding the paper while Holmes remains calm
and unflinching.



                              WATSON
                 But Holmes this is far fetched
                 even for you...everything about the
                 case is crystal clear...the Police
                 have this one figured out...

Holmes examines fingernails bored and shrugs.

                              HOLMES
                 But have they?


Watson waves the paper in front of Holmes face irritated.



                              WATSON
                 YES! It is all there in black and
                 white...and red...and pretty
                 pictures... and worldly news
                 and...why must you always go
                 against the grain?

                              HOLMES
                    Because I'm always right



                              WATSON
                    ...but the evidence against Mr
                    Dog...Digweed?

Holmes shrugs.

                              HOLMES
                    Is circumstantial



                              WATSON
                    I...but...ugh...but it sounds so
                    absurd...he cannot be innocent
                    I...look this is some sort of joke
                    isn't it? I know you Holmes...your
                    trying to string me along to
                    believe something ridiculous as
                    this, only to then pull the rug
                    from under my feet



                              HOLMES
                    No Watson this is no jape or
                    caper...this is a potentially
                    innocent man facing a life
                    sentence for another mans sins...I
                    kid ye not

He pauses as if something has dawned on him as he reconsiders
what he has just said, Watson looks at him puzzled as to why
he stopped talking and is expecting him to continue his
sentence any moment, Miss Blake looks on baffled.

                              HOLMES
                    ...Kid ye......not Kid ye... not...



                              WATSON
                    Oh no here we go



                              HOLMES
                    Kid...Kidye...Kid ye...KIDNEY!

Miss Blake and Watson exchange thoroughly confused
expressions.

                                166

                    **HOLMES**
KIDNEY


                  **MISS BLAKE**
Kidney?


              **WATSON** [JOKINGLY]
Miss Blake I think Holmes has
decided what he wants for lunch…

Watson then ponders on this then decides he actually likes
this idea.

                    **WATSON**
Actually…Steak and Kidney
pie…yes… with mash…and boiled
carrots…and minted peas…could we
have that Miss Blake?

Holmes springs into action and begins pacing in front of the
fireplace.

                    **HOLMES**
NO! That is it…I am sure…Mr.
Digweed had a kidney removed…he
is on Dialysis…now my medical
knowledge on anatomy is not
overtly refined so…WATSON! Have
you purchased a medical reference
tome since our arrival here?


                    **WATSON**
…yes in the front room bookshelf
but what's that got to do with…


              **HOLMES** [INTERUPTS]
Excellent…I need to commit myself
to a few hours of study of it to
ensure I fully understand this
myself…


                    **WATSON**
Why?

Holmes smiles but ignores him then swivels pointing finger to
Miss Blake who jumps slightly alarmed.

                    **HOLMES**
          MISS BLAKE forget about making
          our lunch for a minute


                    **WATSON**
          Wait…what…now hang on a minute


                    **HOLMES**
          I need your assistance in this
          investigation…the both of you


Miss Blake claps hands excited and sits up.


                    **MISS BLAKE**
          When you like where you like!


                    **WATSON**
          Hang on that's my catchphrase

Holmes and Miss Blake exchanges glances then both look at him
puzzled.

                    **HOLMES**
          …I thought it was "The Doctor is
          in the house"


                    **WATSON**
          …you said I wasn't allowed that

Watson goes to open his mouth and argue but decides better of
it and shakes his head resigned knowing there is little point
arguing.

                    **HOLMES**
          Miss Blake…a little research task
          can you look up whom lives at 18
          Gillete Grove…find out who lives
          there…how long they have been
          there… do you need me to write
          that address down?

**MISS BLAKE**

Nooo...I can remember...

Holmes smiles then spins on heels to face Watson.

**HOLMES**

Excellent! Now Watson...you have a
kind and trusting face

Watson looks slightly confused by this.

**WATSON**

I...er...thank you Holmes...but what
did you need me to do?

**HOLMES**

Use it to gain the trust of the
medical profession at the St.
Albans Medical Surgery...for I need
you to pretend to be a doctor

Watson looks insulted by this.

**WATSON**

...I *am* a doctor

Holmes smiles and clasps his hand on Watson's shoulder.

**HOLMES**

Which should just about make up
for the fact you are a terrible
actor! I need you to get in the
inner sanctum and extract the
medical records of Mr. Digweed

**WATSON**

His records...Holmes...why? No, I am
not comfortable with this and...

Before he can finish Holmes has turned on his heels and
quickly paced out of the room shouting.

**HOLMES**
Where's your vigour Watson! I do
not suspect Mr. Digweed will be
all too comfortable if he spends
the rest of his life in jail for
a crime he did not commit...

Miss Blake and Watson watch him stride up the hall into the
front room; they then glance to one another and shrug.

**MISS BLAKE**
I'm not sure what's going on...but
I am really excited to be
involved...

Miss Blake's look of elation changes to confusion.

**MISS BLISS**
Err I don't suppose you caught
the address ...I remember the first
bit 18...95...?...57 no...25...no ...eighty
twelve...Road?

**WATSON**
18 Gillette Grove Miss Blake...

Miss Blake smiles at him jumping up hugging him tightly much
to his dazzled surprise.

**MISS BLAKE**
Oh Thank you John!!! I'll go look
it up right away...

Watson still looks very pleased with himself still dazed.

**WATSON**
...right...well...OK then...

He looks to the table and picks up his cane and hat

**WATSON**
You know what Holmes...I think I
just found my vigour...

He places his hat on and strides out quickly and enthusiastic

170

## SCENE 4A
## EXT:OUTSIDE DOCTORS SURGERY

Watson walks forward to the doctor's surgery with a grim look
on his face muttering.

> **WATSON**
> I don't know why I let you talk
> me into this Holmes…I don't for
> the life of me know how I am even
> going to do this…still…come on
> Watson…stiff upper lip…

FADE TO

## SCENE 4B
## INT:DOCTORS OFFICE

A man in his late 50's sits at his desk dressed in a smart
black blazer and polo neck. He is conducting an imaginary
orchestra with a soft toy when Watson walks in.

> **WATSON**
> Hello there my good man

> **DOCTOR PROCTOR**
> Yes? Hey who said you could come
> into my office…my next
> appointments not till 1:00 pm
> …the time is only 1:30 pm so by
> standard clinic practise really
> you shouldn't be seen for at
> least another hour…get out and go
> pong up the waiting room like the
> rest of them will you

DOCTOR PROCTOR reaches for air spray and sprays it in Watson's
direction.

> **WATSON**
> I…excuse me??? Pong up the…

He sniffs his armpits unsure but finds nothing wrong.

> **WATSON**
> Ok First off what gives you the
> right to be so excessively rude,
> and you are wrong by the way I do
> not...pong...but secondly your
> practise logic makes no sense
> from a business or medical
> standpoint. When I had my surgery
> in Kensington I saw my clients on
> time every time...and I did not
> comment on their scent
> either...ponging or not

Doctor Proctor eyes widen and he becomes apologetic and
friendly instantly.

> **DOCTOR PROCTOR**
> OH...you're a Doctor? OH I am so
> terribly sorry...oh dear...I thought
> you were a patient...had I know I
> would not have been so terribly
> terribly rude and...say...you
> couldn't be a pal and cover for
> me could you ? I need to get my
> wife a birthday present...clean
> forgot!

> **WATSON**
> Wait...cover for you?

Without waiting for a further answer Doctor Proctor rises from
his chair and begins putting on his coat.

> **DOCTOR PROCTOR**
> Wonderful...right...keys are here,
> patient paper records down here
> in these folders...phone there...this
> is a paper clip... don't use it if
> you can help it please oh yes
> pencil sharpener there...

Doctor Proctor looks around again then snatches up a lunch box
holding it close to him protectively.

                    **DOCTOR PROCTOR**
          THESE are MY sandwiches there are
          two and *only two*, one is jam the
          other is peanut butter...you may
          have the one with chocolate
          spread...I think that pretty much
          covers everything you need to
          know


                    **WATSON**
          Hold on, you cannot
          seriously...wait paper patient
          records you say?

Doctor Proctor points to a cabinet on the floor flippantly.

                    **DOCTOR PROCTOR**
          Yes yes in there, right best of
          British luck...don't work too hard
          its not good for your health...now
          what to get my wife...women like
          motorbikes don't they? I have
          always wanted a motorbike......*Vroom
          Vroom*

He begins making motorbike noises and pretending to be turning
a throttle and then drives out on an imaginary bike leaving an
utterly confused Watson to sit down still trying to take in
what has just happened shaking head in disbelief.

                    **WATSON**
          Well...that worked better than
          expected...I am not sure how
          but...least I can get Holmes the
          moonshine files now...I can only
          hope the doctor kept his files in
          better order than his office

He pulls some dockets out of the cabinet and begins leafing
through them.


**SCENE 4c**
**INT: HOMES AND WATSON LIVING ROOM**

Holmes and Miss Blake are seated upon the sofa , Holmes is
deep absorbed in a medical book. Miss Blake is tapping away at
an I-Pad. Holmes frowns at the I-pad then returns to his book.


                    **MISS BLAKE**

Oh wow this is just like Spooks
and I am like the clever
reaserchy one...I should get a lab
coat...and a clip board

Holmes nods but has no clue as to what she is talking about.

                    **MISS BLAKE**
OMG! And finally a reason to buy
some designer spectacles yes!

She squeezes his arm excited and then continues to tap away.

                    **MISS BLAKE**
...carry on...

                                        FADE OUT

## SCENE 5
## EXT: OUTSIDE DOCTORS SURGERY

Watson walks from the surgery concealing the file in his
jacket and glancing around slightly nervously encase anyone
spots him and begins muttering to himself as he goes.

                    **WATSON**
Well Holmes... I don't know why I
have done it...but done it I have...
and

He pauses lowering the file and stares ahead of him mouth open
slightly shocked.

                    **WATSON**
Good gravy...that is not...it cannot
be......

                                        CUT TO

## EXT: STREET BESIDE DOCTORS

MADELINE and REBECCA are walking along street opposite to
Watson. Madeline appears to be on the phone looking irritated
by the conversation she is having.

                    **WATSON** *V/O*
That cannot be who I think it is
can it...

                    **MADELINE**
          What do you mean you got arrested
          for shoplifting hair dye?...NO I
          will not come and get you

Madeline switches off the phone and shakes head.


                    **MADELINE**
          What a moron...anyway can you...go
          over that again please
          Rebecca...the Mr Trade thing...


                    **REBECCA**
          I am telling you Madeline it's a
          dead lead, either Miss Blake got
          the name wrong or it was a lie in
          the first place by Sherlock
          Holmes. I can find no trace of
          any Mr. Les Trade...this friend
          does not exist on any birth or
          electoral roll...in fact the only
          name that even closely resembles
          it I did find would be

She consults a notebook.

                    **REBECCA**
          An Inspector George *Lestrade*...a
          Metropolitan Police Inspector in
          the 19th Century


                    **MADELINE**
          Well THAT'S not going to be him
          now is it

Rebecca snorts and shakes head.

                    **REBECCA**
          No

They continue to walk off down the street.

                                        CUT TO

Watson watches shaking his head in disbelief at what he is
seeing mutters to himself.

>                    **WATSON**
>          That could not have been them,
>          could it? They would not be
>          friends…would they?

He begins to walk off quickly glancing behind him as he goes.


**SCENE 6**
**INT: HOLMES LIVING ROOM**


Holmes is feverishly pacing up and down on the carpet
muttering to him self as Miss Blake watches hands on side
shaking head.


>                    **HOLMES**
>          So you say our deceased scientist
>          had not lived at Gillette Grove
>          for over two years…


>                    **MISS BLAKE**
>          Yep and I confirmed it and
>          everything ringing up the council
>          housing office…Gawd it was so
>          funny though they wanted to know
>          why I wanted to know and I
>          pretended I was a journalist! And
>          they believed me! ME a journalist
>          hah-hah they must have been
>          really thick to fall for someone
>          just pretending to be a
>          journalist

Holmes raises an eyebrow then continues to pace.

>                    **HOLMES**
>          This goes some way to proves Mr.
>          Digweeds innocence…he still
>          thought Travers lived at Gillette
>          Grove…but the killer of course
>          discovered the new address

**MISS BLAKE**

Mr Holmes…must you pace like
that? You are giving me a
headache…I am sure Doctor Watson
won't be too much longer…sit
down…have a break
take a chill pill!

**HOLMES**

NO there is no time for
pills…recreational or medicinal
don't you see Miss Blake!? I have
it I am sure I have it! If I were
to explain it…it may seem
impossible but when you eliminate
the impossible whatever remains
no matter how improbable must be
the truth, all I need is
confirmation of my reasoning…

**SFX : DOOR OPENS**

Watson rushes in looking hot and bothered and strides straight
through the kitchen into the living room. Holmes looks up with
excitement and rushes over.

**HOLMES**

Ah WATSON! Did you get the file?

**WATSON**

Er…yes I did but Holmes listen I
saw…well think I saw rather, one
of the strangest things I…

Holmes has already snatched the file Watson was holding close
to his chest and turned away from him as he flips through the
file.

**HOLMES**

WATSON…how did you get jam on
this?

#### WATSON

Holmes listen...I...wait what...oh well
the Doctor said I could have his
chocolate spread sandwich but
there wasn't actually one so I
presumed he wouldn't mind if I
had the jam one...AND seeing as my
lunch had been prematurely
cancelled I...


#### HOLMES [INTERRUPTS]

Watson that doesn't explain how
you got jam on the file...and...

He pauses and takes a sharp intake of breath and stabs his
finger on the file.


#### HOLMES

YES...I knew it...this confirms my
reasoning's...well done Watson!
Well done Miss Blake...your
assistance has been most
appreciated...now I must go find
Mr. Digweeds fiancé...I believe she
mentioned being at an anti-deer
cull rally today...finally a
legitimate reason to wear my deer
stalker hat

He picks the hat off the table with his cane and goes to rush
out.


#### WATSON

Oh but Holmes! I didn't get to
finish my story


#### HOLMES

It cannot have been that urgent
for you chose to prioritise
telling me some fable
involving...jam sandwiches first...so
I am sure it can wait...

He rushes out of the living room into the kitchen and out as
Watson leans his head out of the door shouting after him.


#### WATSON

That's because you asked me about
it...Holmes!!!

He lets out a dejected sigh and shakes his head wearily trudging back to the sofa where Miss Blake is sitting reading a magazine.

> **WATSON**
> Oh…never mind…I was probably
> wrong anyway…I *normally am…*

Miss Blake looks up from her magazine before patting the space next to her indicating him to sit with her.

Watson shakes his head picks newspaper up from the table and goes to sit next to her still looking rather glum , Miss Blake looks at him feeling slightly sad and puts down her magazine and thinks for a second before standing up and starting to head towards kitchen.

> **MISS BLAKE**
> …how about that Steak and Kidney
> Pie?

Watson perks up and sits more upright.

> **WATSON**
> …with mash?

> **MISS BLAKE**
> With mash

She begins to leave the room as Watson calls after her.

> **WATSON**
> …and carrots?

> **MISS BLAKE**
> …and carrots

Watson looks even more pleased then calls after her again.

> **WATSON**
> …and minted peas?

> **MISS BLAKE**
> …and minted peas

Watson looks rather happier than he did before and nods to himself contented as he picks up the paper once more and reads with a smile on his face.

FADE OUT

**SCENE 7**
**EXT: FOREST**

Open to find a forest ranger MCCREATH surrounded and arguing
with Teresa and a group of supporters turned out behind them
chanting together.

> **PROTESTOR**
> **ONE/TWO/THREE**
> 2-4-6-8 WE ALL THINK THE DEER ARE
> GREAT...2-4-6-8...DON'T LET THEM END
> UP ON YOUR PLATE...

They repeat this chant as Teresa fronts the group chanting
loudest at the ranger who is getting uncomfortable backing up
slightly holding his hands out
as she jabs at his chest.

> **TERESA**
> What makes you think you can kill
> deer like this? How would YOU
> like it if we killed you huh?
> WOULD YOU LIKE THAT

McCreath frowns as Herbert tries to usher Teresa away almost
embarrassed by her aggression.

> **HERBERT**
> ...she didn't mean that...she
> didn't...she's just very
> passionate...Teresa please lets
> keep it civil

> **RANGER MCCREATH**
> Are you threatening me? You
> people are all mad...I like these
> deer just as much as you do

> **TERESA**
> PROVE IT

> **RANGER MCCREATH**
> BUT if we don't do this deer
> cull...there wont be enough food
> for them all and they are getting
> aggressive as it is so they will
> end up killing each other anyway...

180

                              TERESA
          YOU'RE LYING!!!

She lunges forward with her hands raised as if she was going
to attack him only for Holmes to dart in the middle and block
her raised arm.

                              HOLMES
          Actually, I doubt that he is…


                              TERESA
          Mr…MR Holmes…oh…dear…I…am
          um…sorry you had to see that…I


                              HOLMES
          Am very passionate about animal
          rights…yes I had
          noticed…extensively…

McCreath scurries behind Holmes and points a finger at Teresa.

                              MCCREATH
          Keep her away from me, she's
          crazy


                              HOLMES
          Do not fret you are perfectly
          safe I assure you…NOW Miss
          Fairweather, even if our ranger
          friend here WAS lying…he would
          hardly be the only one around
          here to do so


                              TERESA
          What…what do you mean Mr Holmes?
          Do you know something about
          Daniel…is that why you are here?


                              HOLMES
          I know many things about Daniel
          now…and yes it is why I have
          come…


                              181

Holmes surveys the area frowning at the protesters who have
fallen silent since his arrival looking slightly unsure at
him.

                    HOLMES
          Tell me Miss Fairweather...you
          value animal life and wish to
          preserve it...yet I did just hear
          you threaten to remove this mans
          life in order to do so...therefore
          shall I presume the killing of
          one is acceptable to save many?


                    TERESA
          ...heat of the moment...I did...I did
          not mean it

She looks past him to the ranger.

                    TERESA
          I apologize for saying that to
          you...


                    HERBERT
          Look where exactly is this going?
          Are you accusing Teresa? What are
          you playing at?


                    HOLMES
          What am I playing at...well my
          questioning of Miss Fairweather
          has no actual reason Mr. Reeves...I
          suppose you could call it biding
          time and...toying with...you...


                    HERBERT
          What...?


                    HOLMES
          Yes it is interesting how you are
          the least vocal one in this
          protest but the most forthright
          in your actions...a do-er not a
          say-er.

Teresa glances at Herbert confused then back to Holmes.

                    TERESA
          Herbert? Mr. Holmes sorry I don't
          see what this…


                    HOLMES
          Mr. Reeves has taken your
          campaign above and beyond one
          could say…by that I mean of
          course having the lab technician
          disposed of means he has perhaps
          saved animal lives and helped
          prevent future caging of
          animals…but at the cost
          ironically of permanently
          imprisoning your friend in jail
          and the disposal of a human life…

Herbert becomes livid and slightly hysterical.

                    HERBERT
          There is no proof of that AND I
          would NEVER hurt a soul


                    HOLMES
          Mmm…soul maybe not…the human body
          containing said soul…yes…as for
          no proof OH Mr. Reeves you make
          it too easy…I love it when they
          deny it, shall we start with the
          little things, you're a gardener
          by trade…you have access to a
          pitchfork with ease

Herbert laughs and shakes head sneering.

                    HERBERT
          That's pathetic anyone can get a
          pitch fork…you will have to do
          better than that


                    HOLMES
          Challenge accepted…you suffer
          from nosebleeds…but weren't born
          with this…

                                        CUT TO
                                        FLASHBACK


                    183

Teresa shakes head and sighs folding arms

                    TERESA
          ...Herbert you ALWAYS have nose
          bleeds...


                    HERBERT
          Well I haven't always though have
          I...err yes but even so...

                                        FADE RETURN
                                        TO SCENE


                    HOLMES
          Interesting, for when I visited
          Mr. Digweed and leant him a
          handkerchief...

                                        CUT TO
                                        FLASHBACK


Holmes frowns then pats his pockets eventually extracting one
and handing it over to Mr Digweed who takes it and stuffs it
against his nose

                    DIGWEED
          Ah...that's better...sorry man...

He hands it back to Holmes who looks slightly disgusted at it
and gingerly takes it one finger before wrapping in another
tissue and pocketing it.

                                        FADE OUT
                                        RETURN TO
                                        SCENE


Holmes holds out a bloody tissue.


                    HOLMES
          I noticed he too was a sufferer
          of nosebleeds...

                              HERBERT
                    I cant believe we hired this mad
                    man Teresa…what sort of evidence
                    is that?

Holmes smirks and pockets the tissue once more.


                               HOLMES
                    Damning actually but we will come
                    back to why…another of your
                    downfalls when I was visiting Mr.
                    Digweed his dialysis monitor went
                    off

                                                        CUT TO
                                                        FLASHBACK


There is a beep beep noise coming from Mr Digweeds pocket and
he pulls out a small metal device and raises eyebrow

                              DIGWEED
                    Oh its time for my dialysis
                    appointment...I donated one of my
                    kidneys you see...its not a very
                    good one left so yeah I have to
                    have this…say are you the guard
                    that's taking me to the hospital
                    wing today

                                                        FADE BACK
                                                        TO SCENE.


                               HOLMES
                    …the exact same frequency I heard
                    from you Mr Reeves earlier…you
                    also have a dialysis monitor

                                                        CUT TO
                                                        FLASHBACK


                    SFX - beeping alarm

Holmes frowns and looks around and realises its coming from
Herbert who is patting at his jacket.

                              HERBERT
                    So terribly sorry…do please carry
                    on …just a little reminder…but I
                    have time… please do continue

                                                        CUT BACK TO
                                                        SCENE

                                185

                    **HERBERT**
Yes but what has that have to do
with anything?


                    **HOLMES**
Everything...for though you
mentioned kidney transplants you
failed to mention that you
yourself had been the recipient
of one...the alarm gave it away you
too have problems and are on
dialysis thus had to leave
shortly for an appointment
yourself...


                    **HERBERT**
How do you even know I had a
transplant...?

                    **HOLMES**
Because I had Mr. Digweeds
medical records taken from his
surgery...

                                            CUT TO
                                            FLASHBACK


Watson walks from the Doctors Surgery concealing the file in
his jacket and glancing around slightly nervously encase
anyone spots him and begins muttering to himself as he goes

                                            FADE TO
                                            SCENE

                    **HERBERT**
You can't do that...that's illegal

                    **HOLMES**
...mmm...so is murder...anyhow in these
records it named whom Mr.
Digweeds voluntary kidney
donation went too...which
interestingly enough was
actually...you Mr Reeves

                    HERBERT
          ME? It was me? I never knew
          this…well…well…it wasn't a very
          good one as it turns out …I mean
          I still am on dialysis… and…hang
          on…STOP avoiding my question…none
          of this means I killed the man, I
          think your forgetting Daniels
          blood was found at the scene! Mr.
          Travers fought back and spilled
          it

                    HOLMES
          …mmm no actually, it was not
          his…that was yours Mr. Reeves…

                    TERESA
          What?

Teresa stares at Herbert mouth open stunned by this
accusation.

                    HOLMES
          You see the kidney is partly
          responsible for the filtration of
          blood…when you took on his
          kidney…the structure of your
          blood changed slightly to
          adapt…taking on some of the
          memory of Daniels DNA…combined
          with traces of his blood…your
          blood I believe is effectively
          now almost a mimic of his own…

                    TERESA
          So…what are you saying…?

                    HOLMES
          The Police only needed a trace
          element to identify it
          incorrectly as Digweeds for they
          have his DNA but not
          yours…closest match…he's the
          obvious one to blame

Herbert shakes head and snarls.

                    187

                    HERBERT
          Pseudo Science


                    HOLMES
          Which also explains why you
          suffer from nosebleeds…but only
          in more recent years. It's not
          unheard of for a donors recipient
          to take on physical or mental
          anomalies of the donor, A nervous
          tick…a skill in painting…a love
          of French bread…hence you adopted
          Mr. Digweeds nosebleeds…further
          strengthening my theory your body
          has altered structure to his…

Herbert looks to Teresa who is shaking her head in utter
disgust at him and to the protesters who equally are shocked.

                    TERESA
          How could you…you were going to
          let Daniel be jailed for life…

Herbert holds hands up and starts to back away.

                    HERBERT
          He would have wanted it! I saved
          the animals at the lab!!! I just
          finished the job he failed to do…
          he should thank me…YOU ALL SHOULD
          THANK ME


                    HOLMES
          Well…I will thank you if you come
          quietly and…

Herbert bolts pushing past Holmes and flaying his arms in the
air screaming.

                    HERBERT
          YOU'LL NEVER TAKE ME ALIVE


                    HOLMES
          …well you will get no thanks from
          me now…


                         188

**RANGER MCCREATH**
WAIT...NO not that way...that way
leads to the culling ground
site...your going to get yourself
shot...COME ON we have to stop him

Holmes picks up his cane and dashes past McCreath in pursuit
of Herbert.

McCreath paces after them at speed followed by Teresa.

**SCENE 8**
**EXT: INNER FOREST**

Holmes runs through forest, leaping over logs

CUT TO

**EXT: INNER FOREST**

Herbert looking back behind him puffing and panting

CUT TO

**EXT: INNER FOREST**

Teresa and McCreath try to weave their way past trees to
follow.

Eventually Herbert reaches a fern filled field and spins
around crouching slightly to hide puffing and panting out of
breath. He waits a few seconds and then thinking the coast is
clear gets up again only to turn around come face to face with
Holmes.

**HOLMES**
Not to sure where you think your
going...the courts of justice are
back the other way

Herbert jumps back slightly in shock and withdraws a trowel
waving it in front of him.

189

                         HERBERT
              JUSTICE?? You think justice needs
              to be laid down on me? That's
              laughable...I GAVE THE JUSTICE...AND
              THE ONLY WAY POSSIBLE...for years
              for all my beliefs I have
              stickered leafleted...marched and
              participated in bake sales...for
              what? They don't DO anything...NO
              ONE CARES...you can't save tree
              frogs with rice krispie squares


                         HOLMES
              ...but you can by...killing people?

Herbert begins slowly taking a few steps back cautiously
always holding the trowel out as he creates more and more
distance from Holmes.

                         HERBERT
              YES...Well the right people, well
              done Mr. Holmes your as smart as
              they say you are. That's exactly
              it and at the moment YOU are one
              of these people if you stand in
              my way...so here is what's going to
              happen...I am going to walk off
              nice and slowly that a way...and
              YOU are not going to follow
              ...UNDERSTOOD?


                         HOLMES
              ...yes understood...but I really do
              not advise for your safety you go
              that way...

Herbert turns and sneers at him.

                         HERBERT
              Your just trying to stall me
              aren't you...and why can't I go
              this way eh?

Holmes goes to open his mouth but then stops, slowly his eyes
fall to the floor and his head bows , he pauses as Herbert
looks on at him head cocked in uncertainty.

                                             CUT TO
                                             FLASH BACK

                         190

RANGER MCCREATH
WAIT…NO not that way…that way
leads to the culling ground
site…your going to get yourself
shot…we have to stop him

FADE RETURN

Holmes raises his head and pauses once more before looking
Herbert dead on in the eye and shaking his head.

**HOLMES**

…no reason

**HERBERT**

Humph

Herbert takes two steps backwards trowel still trained on
Holmes before turning and running into the forest full pelt.

Holmes watches him with no emotion showing on his face as
McCreath and Teresa come running up from behind.

**RANGER MC CREATH**

MR HOLMES…Mr HOLMES…have you seen
him yet…??? Oh, I pray to God he
didn't go any further than here
or he will be right in the line
of…

*SFX:*
*GUN SHOT (X2)*

*SFX:*
*SHRILL SCREAM*

*SFX:*
*THUMP OF BODY FALLING INTO LEAVES*

Teresa and McCreath exchange horrified expressions and stand
mouths open, Teresa buries her head into her hands.

Holmes stares for a few seconds more before turning and
walking past them and through the forest pausing only to
look around once to the body of Herbert before speaking as he
walks.

                    **HOLMES**
          Come Miss Fairweather…I am going
          to need you to testify
          these…horrific events…

Teresa chews on her lip as if about to cry but nods composes
herself and taking one more look before following Holmes.
McCreath begins to dial his phone and starts speaking to his
control room still in slight state of disbelief.

                    **TERESA**
          …Mr Holmes

Holmes stops but doesn't turn around.

                    **TERESA**
          Mr. Holmes I want you to know…he
          may have been my best friend but
          I do not condone any of his
          actions, I can see now how sick
          he must have been…why else would
          he not have stopped when you
          warned him of the dangers…

Holmes remains stony faced and does not turn.

                    **HOLMES**
          Why else indeed

                    **TERESA**
          But above all Mr Holmes…I am
          sad…sad that Herbert lost sight
          of the whole message and point
          behind our campaigns…that its not
          down to any one of us to decide
          who should live and who should
          die…don't you think Mr Holmes…?

Holmes remains unchanged in his emotion and breathes in deeply

                    **HOLMES**
          What I think…Miss Fairweather…is
          that we have an innocent fiancé
          of yours to free…

He continues to walk off into the distance forest leaving her
to pause, slightly unsure of his answer and look back one last
time at Herbert's body before following on behind him.


                                        FADE OUT


                    **END**

                    192

<u>NO PLACE LIKE HOLMES</u>
<u>SERIES 2 EPISODE FOUR</u>
<u>HATS OFF MR HOLMES</u>


ORIGINAL RUN 22ND DECEMBER - 24TH DECEMBER 2011 (3 PARTS)



<u>CAST</u>



SHERLOCK HOLMES...............................................ROSS K FOAD
DR JOHN H.WATSON...........................................MIKE ARCHER
MISS CHRISTINE BLAKE...............................TAMZIN DUNSTONE
MR ARTHUR SCRUNGE........................................GENE FOAD

MISS BLAKE is putting up tinsel on curtains and Christmas
cards on table as she hums and sings to herself, she
substitutes words she does not know with incoherent murmurings
and changing songs when stuck.

>                    **MISS BLAKE**
>           Silent Night…Holy Night allll… is
>           calm all is bright
>           something…something…holy…um
>           Good King Wensleydale looked out
>           on the…aaaaaand a partridge in a
>           pear tree

HOLMES enters with WATSON and Miss Blake turns to them.

>                    **MISS BLAKE**
>           OH Mr Holmes I

She pauses as she sees Watson then rushes across to embrace
him in a huge hug.

>                    **MISS BLAKE**
>           OH Doctor Watson! Gawd it feels
>           like soo long since I last saw
>           you…you know I had almost
>           forgotten what you looked like!!

Watson looks surprised but pleased as he peels himself out of
her grip.

>                    **WATSON**
>           Why it has been a long time
>           hasn't it Miss Blake but don't
>           worry I am still the same old
>           Watson nothings changed with me……

Miss Blake smiles and then returns to hanging up tinsel.

>                    **MISS BLAKE**
>           Oh Good good…OH Mr Holmes I was
>           thinking!

>                    **HOLMES**
>           [Mutters]
>           That is new…

Watson crosses the room to sit on the sofa and picks up  a
newspaper from the floor.

                        MISS BLAKE
                What is a partridge anyway?



                        HOLMES
                A partridge Miss Blake?
                It is a type of bird, one of
                excellent plumage…commonly eaten
                by the upper classes and well to
                do crowd and contrary to the sing
                song you have just been doing,
                one is unlikely to find them
                nested within a pear tree……do you
                require me to explain what a pear
                tree is?

Miss Blake thinks about it for a few seconds before it dawns
on her she has been insulted.

                        MISS BLAKE
                Noo I DO know what that is…pear
                trees are trees…with pears on
                them…right?

Holmes rolls his eyes then turns his attention to the many
drapes of tinsel sticking down from the ceiling.

                        HOLMES
                Evidently so yes…Miss Blake do we
                really need ALL of these
                Christmas decorations?



                        MISS BLAKE
                Of course we do Mr.Holmes oh your
                not one of those bah humbug
                disbelievers are you?
                One of those that believe in
                monkeys or whatever it is

Miss Blake picks up another strand of tinsel looking for where
to hang it next.

                        WATSON
                Err Miss Blake monkeys are
                scientifically proven to
                exist…and I should know I am a
                Doctor

                              MISS BLAKE
                    So is tinsel




                               WATSON
                    Er yes quite…

Holmes snorts and shakes his head.




                               WATSON
                    You are bored aren't you? I can
                    tell




                               HOLMES
                    [Shrugging]
                    Mm




                               WATSON
                    Your never happy unless you have
                    a case are you

Holmes sighs and begins to pace.

                               HOLMES
                    I abhor the dull routine of
                    existence. I crave for mental
                    exaltation

Miss Blake picks up a magazine and holds it out.

                              MISS BLAKE
                    I know! You should try the Sudoku
                    in here Mr Holmes its like *really*
                    difficult and I bet even you
                    couldn't…

Holmes snatches it from her and takes a cursory glance.

                               HOLMES
                    Starting from Square 1 going in
                    from left to right your answers
                    are 5,7,8,9 and 3




                              MISS BLAKE
                    Oh ok…well done I
                    suppose…right…AHAH but what about
                    the crossword?

                                196

She points to another section on the page.

                    HOLMES
          Child's play, your answers are 1
          Across Charcoal 3 Down
          Buckinghamshire 4 Across
          Stallion...

Miss Blake snatches it back.

                    MISS BLAKE
          Yes I'd quite like to finish it
          myself Mr Holmes thank you very
          much and WELL I'm sorry these
          don't provide any more
          stimulation than the blinkin
          "funny pages" in the newspapers
          might for you

                    HOLMES
          Today's Garfield was repetitious
          and predictable, of course there
          would be no Lasagne in the
          fridge...it is Monday

He turns his attention to Watson.

                    HOLMES
          The Snoopy however was most
          delicious and tickled a funny
          bone for me...who would have
          thought that Lucy would pull the
          football away from Charlie Brown
          just before he kicked it causing
          him to fall flat on his back...it
          was most humorous...you should
          really read it Watson...

                    MISS BLAKE
          Well so glad to hear that

Watson begins searching through paper.

                    **WATSON**
          What you need is a good case…here
          I can bet I find you something of
          interest in here


                    **HOLMES**
          HMPH


                    **WATSON**
          What about this? Mysterious fire
          at Lady Frempongs Mansion
          residence in Kensington, you
          could investigate who did that!

Holmes rolls eyes and continues to pace.

                    **HOLMES**
          Sigh…insurance job


                    **WATSON**
          Oh come on Holmes you can not
          possibly know that


                    **HOLMES**
          The Financial times six days ago,
          Frempongs shares plummeted to a
          time low, his company is in ruin
          therefore it was only a matter of
          time till they did that…case
          closed

Watson blinks a few times in disbelief then shakes head
returning to looking through newspaper.

                    **WATSON**
          Ok…fine ooh here "CAT-Napped"
          Mr Fluff Boo the prize persian
          has again gone missing and its
          owners are appealing for…


                    **HOLMES**
          NO!

                        WATSON
            Very well…

Holmes sighs again.

                        HOLMES
            Oh give up Watson! There are no
            interesting cases to be found, I
            think I need a walk…clear my
            mind…Miss Blake will you fetch my
            cane and top hat?


                        MISS BLAKE
            Oh right yes good idea…wont be
            two ticks

Miss Blake scurries away exiting the room leaving Holmes
looking baffled at a hanging green spring decoration.

                        HOLMES
            …Watson what is this?


                        WATSON
            Decoration Holmes


                        HOLMES
            But why?

Miss Blake returns bounding through the door cheerily.

                        MISS BLAKE
            Here you go

She hands him the cane then proceeds to pull a Santa Claus hat
onto his head.

                        HOLMES
            …What is this?


                        MISS BLAKE
            A Christmas hat…I thought it
            would be more fun

Holmes pats his head looking very worried until his face
breaks into annoyance.

                              HOLMES
                    Well you thought WRONG didn't
                    you!

He flings the hat off his head and into her face before
striding out of the room muttering and grumbling.


                              WATSON
                    [Calling after him]
                    Christmas Spirit Holmes!


                              HOLMES
                    [Shouting back]
                    BAH!

Watson shrugs and pulls a brown paper bag from his jacket.

                              WATSON
                    Oh Miss Blake…would you like a
                    hum bug?


                            MISS BLAKE
                    Oooh yes please lovely…

She dashes over to Watson and takes one from the packet
popping into her mouth before returning to putting up more
tinsel.

Watson picks up the paper once more and opens it to the coffee
break pages.

                              WATSON
                    [Sniggering]
                    Hmm…Oh Holmes does not know what
                    he is talking about; today's
                    Garfield is *most* amusing

                                                      FADE OUT



**SCENE 1B**
**EXT: RIVER SIDE PARK**

Holmes is strolling along when he spies a white cowboy style
hat overturned on a bench. He stares at it puzzled and
approaches it picking it up and looking around him as if for
the owner.

Seeing no one around he flips it over and then his eyes flash
intrigued as he takes out his magnifying glass and runs it
over a red stain, he then brushes his finger on it and touches
his lips.


                        HOLMES
            Blood…



                                        FADE OUT


SCENE 2
INT: FRONT LIVING ROOM

                                        FADE IN

Holmes sat at the table facing the wall back to Miss Blake.
Miss Blake sits at the far side of the living room sat on the
sofa with Doctor Watson, she has the white cowboy hat in her
hands she is turning over and examining with a look of
confusion. Watson is also looking at it with some confusion.


                        HOLMES
            Well Miss Blake are you going to
            put it on your head?
            Alternatively, perhaps you are
            merely contemplating using it to
            give yourself a bowl cut?
            If you want my personal opinion,
            I advise against it for you would
            look most ridiculous

She looks up and almost drops the hat looking wide-eyed and
astonished.

                        MISS BLAKE
            What…how did you know I was
            looking at the hat…you must be
            magic…like in them Harry Potter
            Films…have you seen them!



Holmes spins around in his chair to face Watson and lifts the
shiny coffee pot in front of him.

                        HOLMES
            No no only a well polished coffee
            pot in front of my person

                    WATSON

        Oh I see, it was a trick, why you
        really had me fooled for a minute
        Holmes...


                   MISS BLAKE

        OH a trick...like the TV show with
        that Derren Brown...have you seen
        that? There was this one time
        when he...


                    HOLMES

        [Interrupting]
        What happened to me being magic?
        AHH well fame comes fame goes

Watson picks up the cowboy hat.

                    WATSON

        So is this your new hat then
        Holmes?


                    HOLMES

        HAH...Watson! You know my style
        rises up such vulgar headgear, no
        no that is something I found in
        the park...initially I foolishly
        had fears of foul play because of
        the blood...

Miss Blake looks at in horror as realises there is a stain on
it and throws it to Watson who also jumps back from it.

                   MISS BLAKE

        [Shrieking]
        BLOOD!!!


                    HOLMES

        But after some very simple
        initial enquires...there is no
        actual cause for alarm...the owner
        has been traced and contacted and
        will be on his way here shortly

Miss Blake wipes hands on sofa.

                    MISS BLAKE
But…but there's blood! How can
you be sure the owners not dead


                    HOLMES
Did I not just say I had
contacted him?


                    MISS BLAKE
Well yes but you COULD yeah…but
you COULD have meant you got your
mate Lee Spiritualist to do it by
a séance or Ouji board…Ahh see I
am picking up your logical
thinking method…thing, how is Lee
anyway? Do you think he would
want to come over for Christmas
dinner?…I think he would

She stands up walks across to the table and starts trying to
envision it pointing to the seats.

                    MISS BLAKE
You could go there…and I can be
here…and then he can sit there
and


                    HOLMES
[Interrupts]
Miss Blake…Miss Blake your losing
the trail of thought…and once
again no he is not dead I assure
you


Miss Blake looks disappointed and shuffles back to the sofa
sitting down.

                    HOLMES
Now then Miss Blake…here is a
game if you so believe you are
picking up my "logical thinking
method…thing" apply it…come on
you two what kind of man do you
think has a hat like this?

                    **MISS BLAKE**
          Ah a game! Now you're on…but if
          *we* win though you have to get me
          a really really good Christmas
          present…


                    **HOLMES**
          Mm…very well…try me


Miss Blake squeals with delight then begins running her hands
over the hat turning it over a few times.

                    **MISS BLAKE**
          Ok here goes…lets see …lets
          see…the owner[Peers inside] has a
          bad case of dandruff…

Miss Blake passes to Watson who leans in closer and takes a
sniff.

                    **WATSON**
          He must like Aniseed Sweets

Miss Blake turns it around and holds it out in front of her.

                    **MISS BLAKE**
          And most obvious of all…he must
          be a cowboy! There you have it
          Mr. Holmes…your man is an aniseed
          loving dandruff suffering cowboy…

She smiles at Watson and they both then turn to face Holmes.

                    **WATSON**
          Well Holmes how did we do?


                    **HOLMES**
          OH excellent application of
          methods…excellent…one could even
          say "magic" I can see how you
          came to those conclusions

Miss Blake squeals in delight and nudges Watson.

                    **HOLMES**
          You are of course both completely
          and utterly wrong though

Miss Blake folds arms in a huff.

                        WATSON
          [Irritated]
          What? Well who do YOU think he is
          then?

Watson throws the hat towards the direction of Holmes who
catches it in one hand.

                        HOLMES
          First off Miss Blake…the dandruff
          is too thick and crumbly a
          texture…it is clearly plaster,
          Watson the aniseed you think you
          smell is in fact varnish…both
          have a rather disgusting smell,
          and as for being a
          cowboy…well…how many of those do
          you see galloping around on
          horseback in London these days?


                        MISS BLAKE
          Well who else would have a cowboy
          hat other than a cowboy?


                        HOLMES
          Someone who is brash, cocky and
          wishes to emit an authoritative
          swagger…


                        WATSON
          …are you sure it is not yours
          then?

Miss Blake and Watson share a laugh as Holmes looks grim
faced.

                        HOLMES
          Your developing a very porky
          sense of humour Watson…I would do
          well to learn to guard myself
          from……no no as I was saying, if
          we combine these character traits
          with the evidence of construction
          work  …I would say he would be a
          builder in his fifties…who also
          holds a seasonal job on the side,
          an abattoir perhaps

                              WATSON
                    Oh you can't possibly know all
                    that



                               SFX:
                    KNOCKING AT DOOR

All three turn to face door.

                              HOLMES
                    Oh no? We shall see…Miss Blake if
                    you could please

He motions to the direction of the kitchen and Miss Blake hops
up from sofa.

                            MISS BLAKE
                    Oh, yes of course Mr. Holmes

Miss Blake exits.

Holmes turns to Watson once again and shakes head.

                              HOLMES
                    [Sneering]
                    Aniseed Watson?



                              WATSON
                    Abattoir Holmes?




                                                        FADE OUT




SCENE 3
INT: LIVING ROOM

A man wearing scruffy clothes in his fifties with a builder's
tool set strapped around his waist and carrying a toolbox
lumbers in and followed by Miss Blake.



                            MISS BLAKE
                    Do go through…

Holmes and Watson are now standing and cast a curious glance over to him as he proceeds to put his toolbox down on the table before sticking his hand out towards them.

> **ARTHUR SCRUNGE**
> Mr O'use? My name is Arfur Scrunge…got a message you found me 'at

Holmes and Scrunge shake hands.

> **HOLMES**
> Er…Holmes…and this is my friend and colleague Doctor Watson

> **WATSON**
> It is a pleasure to meet you Mr.Scrunge…

> **ARTHUR SCRUNGE**
> Like wise Doctor Wotsit

> **HOLMES**
> And *here* is your hat

Holmes hands him the hat and a look of great joy comes over Mr. Scrunges face as he holds it out examining it.

> **ARTHUR SCRUNGE**
> Cor Ta very much…this is decent of you Mr Ouse… real decent, musta forgot about it while in the midst of plastering this wall in the park right and varnishing the bench when my mate Ron asked me for a six by four .
> "Six by four?" I said "yeah six by four" he said, you sure it was six by four you wanted I axed him, and he said yeah six by four

Miss Blake and Holmes exchange glances confused.

#### ARTHUR SCRUNGE
So I says six by four and then he
says yeah six by four…so I go
away and make this six by four
and I give it him and he goes
what's this! I says six by four,
he says no it ain't I wanted six
by four to fit a left corner not
a right corner…right! So, I says
you never said that and so you
want me to cut a six by four left
then!

#### HOLMES
Right…

#### ARTHUR SCRUNGE
No NO that's the point it were a
left he wanted…

Holmes casts a cheeky glance to Watson before turning back to
Scrunge and clapping hands together quickly trying to move
matters along.

#### HOLMES
WELL…yes that is fantastic Mr.
Scrunge

#### ARTHUR SCRUNGE
I am so grateful to you Mr 'Ouse
for finding me titfer…this hat
cost me sixty quid you know and
now I don't have to fork out for
a new one…Christmas hits me hard
you see what with the missus's,
me four ex wives, twelve
children…their twelve children
and Thump of course

Watson raises an eyebrow and hesitantly asks.

#### WATSON
…Thump?

#### ARTHUR SCRUNGE
THUMP…the dog of course…so yeah
that's why I gotta do a

Xmas season job at Mr. Bacons
abattoir s'alrigh…cash in
hand……bit messy though

Arthur Scrunge turns over the hat and points to the
bloodstain.

### ARTHUR SCRUNGE
Look pigs blood on me hat! Eh
can't be helped got to be done

He places the hat on his head and adjusts it on his head.

### ARTHUR SCRUNGE
Right…thanks again eh…I'm now off
down to dip my beakle into the
treacle down the weasel and stoat
pub


### HOLMES
Something to celebrate indeed…BUT

Mr. Scrunge who was going to leave turns back around again
glancing at Holmes.

### HOLMES
Mr Scrunge, while I often take
cases on for nothing in the name
of justice which is its own
reward, I do not operate a
charity therefore in this
instance I am going to have to
enquire as to my payment. For
there is the time spent on the
leg work, investigation and
personal expenses incurred… all
together I will say eighty pounds

Arthur Scrunge nods and pulls out an envelope counting out
notes.

### ARTHUR SCRUNGE
Right…and how much is that for
cash

Mr. Scrunge winks and taps his nose, Holmes and Watson look at
one another puzzled.

### HOLMES
…it is…eighty pounds…

                              ARTHUR SCRUNGE
                    Ah right right fair enough
                    ok…here you go

He hands over the cash to Holmes who in turn hands him back a
small piece of paper.


                              HOLMES
                    Thank you, and here is your
                    receipt



                              ARTHUR SCRUNGE
                    [Clueless]
                    What's a receipt?

Holmes places hands on Mr Scrunge and begins to guide him out
of the door.


INT: HALLWAY

                              HOLMES
                    Yes well thank you Mr. Scrunge so
                    much for your time good day now
                    enjoy your hat…do not go losing
                    it mind as it is very chilly
                    out…good day

Holmes opens the front door.

                              ARTHUR SCRUNGE
                    Oh right…well fanks again Mr Ouse
                    and do come see me if you need
                    any plastering done



                              HOLMES
                    Oh I will

Arthur Scrunge is pushed gently of the door.

                              ARTHUR SCRUNGE
                    Or Ron

                              HOLMES
                    Yes or Ron…

Holmes shuts the door, shakes his head then walks back to
living room.

Holmes dusts his hands off as he enters where Miss Blake and
Watson are still seated staring in amazement.

                    **WATSON**
          Holmes…did that man just give you
          eighty pounds for returning his
          sixty pound hat?


                    **HOLMES**
          He did indeed


                    **WATSON**
          And He WAS a builder in his
          fifties's with a seasonal job in
          an abattoir…wait you didn't say
          how you knew about that part?


                    **HOLMES**
          Elementary…building is a trade in
          which the work is not always
          constant depending on contracts,
          so taking additional tasks would
          be likely given the season on top
          of the fact I identified pigs
          blood on the hat, which by the
          way has a similar make up to
          human…a temporary slaughter job
          would be an obvious conclusion


                    **MISS BLAKE**
          Wow…


                    **HOLMES**
          [Irritated]
          I am insulted you sound surprised


                    **MISS BLAKE**
          Well I never…well tut…
          Awww Guess we didn't win after
          all…

211

Holmes smirks and begins counting the cash.

> **HOLMES**
> No you did not but never the
> less, I suppose I am feeling
> "Christmassy" so I shall still
> get you a "really really good
> Christmas present"

Miss Blake claps hands together excited.

> **MISS BLAKE**
> REALLY!!!

> **HOLMES**
> Yes…really…NOW…If you two will
> excuse me I wish to indulge in
> one my other past times. I shall
> sit in the front room… in the
> dark and brood moodily for no
> reason…but I shall also take some
> time to consider what I shall get
> you too

> **MISS BLAKE**
> You know I like shoes right?

Holmes raises eyebrows then spins on heels before walking out.

> **MISS BLAKE**
> [Calling after him]
> Shoooooooooooooes!!!

Miss Blake smiles at Watson then picks up a magazine on the
floor.

> **MISS BLAKE**
> Right well…while I have got some
> peace and quiet for once I think
> I will do the quiz in my
> magazine…he might have done the
> Sudoku and crossword but at least
> you didn't finish that Mr Holmes!

She opens to the right page in the magazine then turns to
Watson once more.

> **MISS BLAKE**
> …I hope he does get me some
> shoes…

                        WATSON
        [Baffled]
        But you have got about twenty
        pairs of shoes?

Miss Blake sighs and shakes her head.

                      MISS BLAKE
        Don't remind me of my pitifully
        small collection of shoes…

She returns her attention to the magazine concentrating hard.

                      MISS BLAKE
        Right…fragrant herb that goes
        with tomatoes


                      HOLMES   V/O
        BASIL!!!

Miss Blake frowns and mutters writing it down.

                      MISS BLAKE
        …yes thank you…right then next
        question…"Another word for
        fury?"…hmm


                      HOLMES  V/O
        WRATH!!!


Miss Brake mutters and shakes head.


                      MISS BLAKE
        Hmph…yes thank you…*again*…well you
        wont get the next one…"The solid
        connective tissue of mammals?"
        hmm…


                      HOLMES  V/O
        BONE!!!


Miss Blake lets out a very irritated sigh folds up her
magazine throws it to the floor with force then leans back on
sofa arms folded with a face of thunder muttering to herself.

                              **MISS BLAKE**
                    John in that box…do we have any
                    holly left?

Watson glances at the cardboard box next to him and pulls it
up to his lap.


                              **WATSON**
                    Err yes a whole bagful it would
                    seem…surely your not doing MORE
                    decorating are you Miss
                    Blake…this place is looking more
                    and more like St Nicholas's
                    Grotto




                              **MISS BLAKE**
                    No

She picks up a bag from inside box and stands up walking
across the room.

                              **MISS BLAKE**
                    I have other housework to do…such
                    as *making Mr.Holmes's bed*

She stomps off out of the room leaving Watson looking a little
uncertain; he shakes his head dismissing what he thinks she is
up too and returns to his newspaper.

                                                    FADE OUT


**SCENE 3**
**INT: HOLMES BEDROOM**

Holmes is in his dressing gown getting ready to get into bed
he stretches and yawns.

                              **WATSON V/O**
                    Good night Holmes




                              **HOLMES**
                    Yes Good night Watson…




                              **WATSON V/O**
                    Good night Miss Blake

**MISS BLAKE V/O**

Good night Doctor Watson...good
night Mr. Holmes


**HOLMES**

[Sleepily mutters]
Yes...good night Miss Blake...

Holmes turns off bedside lamp then settles down.

                                                    CUT TO


EXT: OUTSIDE OF HOUSE

There is a brief period of complete silence as the snow slowly
drifts down from the night sky.

**HOLMES V/O**

AGGGGGGHHHHHHH!

                                                    CUT TO


INT: HOLMES BEDROOM

Holmes scrambles out of bed in and throws back the covers to
reveal a large sprig of holly underneath his bed.

**HOLMES**

What the...holly????


**MISS BLAKE V/O**

[Cackling]
Hahahaha MERRY CHRISTMAS
MR.HOLMES!!!

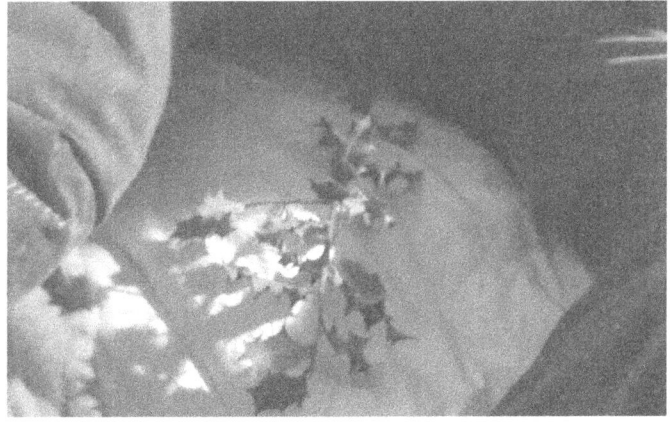

END

# THE GREAT SHERLOCK HOLMES DEBATE 3 SKETCH

This sketch  was made by request of MX Publishing to promote the upcoming "Great Sherlock Holmes Debate 3".

The Great Debate Sketches are effectively *Non-NPLH Canon* as Holmes and Watson have open acknowledgement of other Sherlock Holmes media productions based upon them as well as breaking 4th wall to note that there is an audience watching them.

This time around the debate focused on teams presenting and arguing the case for their favourite short Sherlock Holmes story from ACD's Canon. It also included a bonus event of a lesson in deduction from mentalist Joe Riggs (also available on website).

When it came to creating the promo sketch it seemed fitting to incorporate Holmes dissatisfaction with the way Watson covered his cases in writing and see's the duo arguing over which story is the best one written.

This one was great fun to film; there is something very oddly satisfying about goading Watson on the ludicrous notion of the quantity of geese affects the quality of a story just to see his world-weary expressions of defeat and exasperation.

## INT: HOLMES/WATSON FRONT ROOM

HOLMES and WATSON are sitting upon the sofa, scattered around them are bundles of papers and various Holmes books and pastiches.

Holmes has his eyes closed peacefully clearly deep contemplating something while Watson has pen and papers in front of him, head down scribbling.

After around 10 seconds, Watson stops and places the lid on his pen and begins playing with it his hand.

> ### WATSON
> Holmes? Can I seek your opinion
> on something Holmes?

> ### HOLMES
> Sought away my dear friend by all
> means for without asking we would
> never know anything

Watson smiles and nods then goes to open his mouth only to be cut off by Holmes.

> ### HOLMES
> That being said! Good observation
> almost does away with asking…NOW
> let me see…going from the vast
> array of books you have out…the
> pen in hand…the reams of
> paper…the unsure hesitant look
> upon your face…your going to ask
> me something about the stories
> you write but unsure how I will
> react?

> ### WATSON
> Uh…well yes, I was actually…I was
> wondering which of the stories of
> your adventures was your
> favourite?

> ### HOLMES
> Favourite?

                    WATSON
          Well yes…you know…the one you
          like best…


                    HOLMES
          …best?

Watson picks up a book lying on the sofa and gazes at it.

                    WATSON
          Is it "The Adventure Of The Blue
          Carbuncle" perhaps? You know that
          was the one in which we found the
          missing blue carbuncle in the
          goose


                    HOLMES
          Oh is that which one it was…I
          would never have guessed going
          from your choice of title. No
          Watson I did not like that write
          up…FAR too many geese for my
          liking


                    WATSON
          …but Holmes there were geese


                    HOLMES
          Yes but not quite as many as
          that…had you perhaps included
          less geese then I would have gone
          with that one…have you done the
          Giant Rat Of Sumatra yet?


                    WATSON
          Ah no! But I was thinking of do…

                              **HOLMES**
             [Interrupting]
             Good! Don't ever, now then
             favourite story of one of my
             adventures mmm I think I would
             have to go for The Gloria Scott,
             The Lions Mane, The Blanched
             Solider or The Musgrave Ritual

Watson puts tongue against cheek and makes a clicking noise.

                              **WATSON**
             ......all...excellent choices...very good
             ones yes...but...Holmes...THOSE...are *all
             the ones YOU wrote*

Holmes shrugs.

                              **HOLMES**
             Yes...and they are my
             favourites...debate closed

Holmes stands up ready to leave only for Watson to follow him
up as they face one another squaring off.

                              **WATSON**
             No Holmes it's far from closed
             actually

                              **HOLMES**
             No? Oh who else's opinion are you
             going to ask? Miss Blake? OH Yes
             I am sure she would offer some
             genius insight on the matter

                              **WATSON**
             No...I am going to ask
             [Nods to Camera]
             ...them

                              **HOLMES**
             ...them?

Watson points again.

                              **WATSON**
             Them

**HOLMES**
[Looks to camera] Them? OH
*Them*...Oh not *them* again...it's
surely not that time *again*


**WATSON**
I am afraid so Holmes

Holmes sits down on sofa hands in head shaking in despair.

Watson smiles and sits himself back down patting Holmes on the
back.

**WATSON**
There...There...There...

FADE OUT TO
FULL GSHD3
DETAILS
TEXT
DISPLAY

**END**

# SHERLAPOOLAZA PROMO
## SKETCH

"THE SHERLAPOOLZA SKETCH" was a special promotional mini episode made upon the request of the popular all female podcast team "The Baker Street Babes" to promote "SHERLAPOOLZA 2012".

This was a special event day they were organizing taking place in the Prince Charles Cinema in London in which the entire 2nd season of the BBC's modern day SHERLOCK series was shown on the big screen. The day also consisted of special guest speakers and a quiz.

In a similar fashion to The Great Debate Sketches, the Sketch is considered *"Non-NPLH Canon"* for the fact that Holmes and Watson break the fourth wall to acknowledge viewers as well as recognizing there are television shows and films based on them; In the main shows universe other entities of Holmes do not exist.

**Aired 16th October 2012**

## INT:HOLMES AND WATSONS LIVING ROOM

Open to find HOLMES and WATSON on the sofa, Watson is holding a newspaper and reading it while Holmes tangles himself up with ball of string wrapping it around his arm muttering to himself deep in concentration.

                    WATSON
        Here Holmes look at this I...

He pauses noticing Holmes wrapping a load of string all over the sofa creating a huge mess and examining an end with a magnifying glass.

                    WATSON
            Holmes might I be permitted to
            ask what exactly it is that you
            are doing?

Holmes looks up briefly as if surprised by Watson's presence and was unaware he was even there.

                    HOLMES
            Mmm? Oh Watson! You are of course
            familiar with the age old retort
            of ambiguity "How long is a piece
            of string"

Watson thinks about this for a second and appears deep in thought but cannot fathom what this has to do with anything.

                    WATSON
        …yes…

                    HOLMES
            It is such a fobbing answer is it
            not? I can not stand such
            philosophical foolish musings…you
            know my stance on guess work…why
            can there not be a definitive
            answer…I am sure mathematics and
            science can provide one and when
            they do I shall write a monograph
            on the subject

Watson raises his eyebrows and clearly cannot see why this would be remotely useful but is politely supportive to the idea.

**WATSON**

Well that's…riveting Holmes…but while I wait for THAT article to appear in the paper here is an interesting one…you recall *The Great Debate* of earlier this year where 2 opposing factions debated the merits of the Television show against the feature films based on the stories I have been writing of our adventures


**HOLMES**

Oh yes *that*…what of it?


**WATSON**

Well look here, a group of ladies known as the Baker Street Babes have arranged it so that the Prince Charles Cinema in London will be hosting a special day out where one can purchase a ticket and watch the second season of the BBC's television adaptations in its entirely


**HOLMES**

The cinema…


**WATSON**

Yes, you know it is like the television thing…only big! It is like a public spectacle


Holmes waves his hand flippantly.

**HOLMES**

Yes yes We have been here for 3 years now Watson I am familiar with the concept of the cinema…goodness knows Miss Blake has waxed lyrical about them enough…what ever is your point?

                    **WATSON**
Well, like I said there is this
event where one can watch the
series on a big screen as well as
partake in a viewing of a Q and A
session with special guests …do
you fancy going?


                    **HOLMES**
Do…I…fancy…going?


                    **WATSON**
Yes…there is a goody bag involved
too

Holmes makes no response and just stares at Watson.

                    **WATSON**
Oh come on Holmes I do not
understand this fierce aversion
to modern day developments…look I
am just a traditionalist as you
are but people are going to get
suspicious of our past if we
avoid all modern ways of life
entirely


                    **HOLMES**
I am not going and that is final,
if you insist on going you will
have to go on your own

Holmes stands up to leave signalling the end of the
conversation but Watson throws his paper down and rises from
his seat to face Holmes.

                    **WATSON**
…Oh I will be going Holmes…but I
will certainly not be doing so
alone


                    **HOLMES**
Oh really? Well with Miss Blake
being away in Dover visiting her
brother who else are you going to
invite mm??

Holmes smirks confident he has won the argument but after a short pause, Watson points quickly to the front of camera breaking fourth wall.

                        **WATSON**
        Them...

                        **HOLMES**
        Them...?

                        **WATSON**
        Yes them if they buy a ticket
        they can come too

                        **HOLMES**
        OH for Goodness sake not *them*
        again WHY DO YOU KEEP LETTING
        THESE PEOPLE INTO OUR HOUSE!!!

Holmes shoves the string into Watson's hands irritated and turns stalking out the room.

                        **HOLMES**
        Well I hope you and THEM enjoy
        it! The answers 17 by the way!

Watson smiles to himself and sits down still and begins to try and wrap the string back up with difficulty.

                        **WATSON**
        Holmes! You have tangled Miss
        Blake's skein oh I mean string!
        Her good string! Come back here
        and untie it this instant

He passes a glare at the direction Holmes left before turning his attention to the string again.

                        **WATSON**
        Good Lord! A frayed end!

                        **END**

# ART GALLERY

Over the years we have had some beautiful title cards and fan art works created for the series, some of which I would like to share with you.

**Red VS Right by Alex Funken 2013**

**Creature In The Rye Title Card –**

**Main Website Picture - Jordan Mooney - 2011**

Morstan vs milverton title card- eldred ryan – 2012

One Pipe Problem – Eldred Ryan 2012

A Mural of Mycroft – Alexandra Funken - 2013

## 2013 and Beyond

I cannot truly make a full reflection upon the year 2013 obviously. Nevertheless, I can say for the first time in a very long time that there is touch of excitement, anticipation and hope in the air for what might be next for me and No Place Like Holmes. I think the very fact this book even exists is partly why I feel that.

What I do know though is this year will bring a fourth series of NPLH that will be its best looking, the best sounding and the most exciting and shocking to date. I do know Howard and I will continue to collect and present the autographs of Holmes and Watson actors new and old for you to see upon the site. I do know there are hundreds of Holmes books out there and even more forthcoming that I will continue to review and let you know which ones might be worthy of your attention .

But also at the time of this book's publication we will be on the brink of the Great Sherlock Holmes Debate 4 as well as The Sherlock Holmes Past and Present Summit at the UCL London . Both events will be covered by myself for those not lucky enough to attend to be able to see.

My three primary goals when I started NPLH was to provide a platform for actors to help them gain exposure and develop on their own paths, to get my work as a script writer more exposure and above all else – to have fun. Going on the journey I have been down, reading the comments and messages that I have and the laughs myself and many others have shared I can safely say my original goals have been achieved to some degree plus a hell of a lot more that I never imagined I would do.

The right people have come into my life and the wrong people have left it through the course of this adventure, NPLH has given my life so much purpose, opportunities and enjoyment and I cannot wait to see what happens next.

Perhaps you will like to come with me and see, but best bring your service revolver if you do. Who knows what is out there waiting.

Games Afoot!

- Ross K Foad

May 2013.

## Acknowledgements

There are many people I would like to thank from over the years who have each in their own way contributed, supported and encouraged the growth of *No Place Like Holmes* and allowed it to become the unique Holmes media entity it is today.

As any creative soul of any nature will likely tell you, often it is easy to question what the point of doing ones art is. Whether anyone would truly notice if we were to pack it in all and cease further activity?

Thankfully, despite this theme being a frequent unwelcome visitor to my thoughts attic I refused to give in.

This is partly because the alternative was unthinkable. A life where I could not express my creative thoughts is no life at all for me, the other reason stems from the overwhelming support certain individuals have shown for my works and projects.

Every comment or message I have received or certain actions of others have continued to fuel my love for this project and given reason to wanting to carry it on.

To these people a simple thank you seems insufficient…but all the same…it would be rude not to!

To my **Mother** and **Father** for endless support to my works and of course for their brilliant performances in the show themselves as Mrs. Hudson and whichever the hell odd ball character I have written for my Dad this month.

To my very own dear Watson **Michael Archer,** there could be no more fitting companion to the temperament of my Holmes portrayal than Michaels outstanding actor skills allow. Any warmth you view on screen (*when I am not berating or being snide*) from myself to him is entirely genuine and for good cause too.

To **Steve Emecz**, for plucking me from the obscurities of the interwebs and bringing me to the more mainstream awareness of Sherlock Holmes communities. For allowing me to continue to bring the Great Sherlock Holmes Debates to the Holmesian community in video format and of course for having the faith in me to allow this book's publication. This man revolutionized the Holmes pastiche growth and is easily the worlds greatest publisher

To my modern day fictional housekeeper and longest running cast member **Tazmin Dunstone,** who once said she would continue to do the show even if we were the only two people who watched it. The fact there is this book Tamz makes me think maybe more people than just you and I are watching this now? With out her off screen and equally on screen support the series would have struggled to get much further during the second series. It is a joy to work with such talent.

To **Kelsey Williams**, a continuously strong presence of support and equally strong performance. I love you dearly even if you and your Red Headed League are so very desperate to bring about my demise …

To **Amy Louise Brunskill** for her support and keeping me (relatively) sane during the writing process for this book, in a strange way if I did not create No Place Like Holmes, I might have never met you and if I had never met you, there would be someone very special missing from my life.

To the other villains **Adrian Charlton** and **Angela Holmes** for their enthusiasm loyalty and amazing acting skills. Villains have never been more loved!

In addition, let us not forget Brother Mycroft **James Ian Gray** and **Lexi Wolfe**, both whom deserve much cake.

Then my real life brother **Patrick Foad** who everyone else in the world calls Patt, thank you for encouraging me to start this in the first place and saving the day for the pilot episode *(did I mention my brother won second place in the British Moustache and Beard Championships?)*

I must also give special mention to **Howard Ostrom**, for allowing me to bring his outstanding collection into the NPLH fold for the world to see, his unrivalled knowledge of Holmes actors on screen and his continued support and promotion of my projects.

**Professor Marino Alvarez** for inducting me as an honorary member of the *Nashville Three Pipe Problem Scholars,* a teacher I wish I could have had back in my own school days.

*Phil Growick* because he *is Phil Growick.*

**Anthony Horowitz** for being my inspiration as a writer and for creating a Six Napoleon rated book, **Sir Arthur Conan Doyle** for of course creating the wonderful series that is Professor Challenger *(it's what he would have wanted to be credited for.....)* .

The Ryan brothers **Eldred** and **Devon** for their support and Eldred's awesome title cards . **Jordan Mooney** for the early title cards and the iconic "LE HMPH" grumpy Napoleon statue illustration.

Then there are certain fans that specially come to mind for being continuously vocal in their appreciation and support. Their comments and messages have been instrumental into learning to believe in myself and why it is so worth doing at the end of the day ; **Anne Butler, Paul Spiring, Amy Holleworth, Leslie Davis , Alex Funken, Fiona Jane Brown, Pat Webar, Claire Ellul, Jacqueline Applegate, Jennie Patton, "Holmes Fever" Tom Eu, Meg Zhan,"MrCrassuswild", Kirby Clarke, Dicky Neely, Joe Riggs, "Sneverussnapus", Alistair Duncan .**

And of course finally....**YOU** for reading this book.

**THANK YOU.**


## Contact
If you want to express an interest for a role in the show, want to gain crew experience, have a book you would like to suggest I review or want to send me or just want to say Hi!

Feel free to get in touch. I would love to hear from you.
rosskfoad@gmail.com

23 Windsor Road
Kingston Upon Thames
Surrey
KT2 5EY
ENGLAND.

*"Without Undershaw, there would be no Sherlock Holmes"*

Please show your support by liking the Facebook page.

https://www.facebook.com/saveundershaw

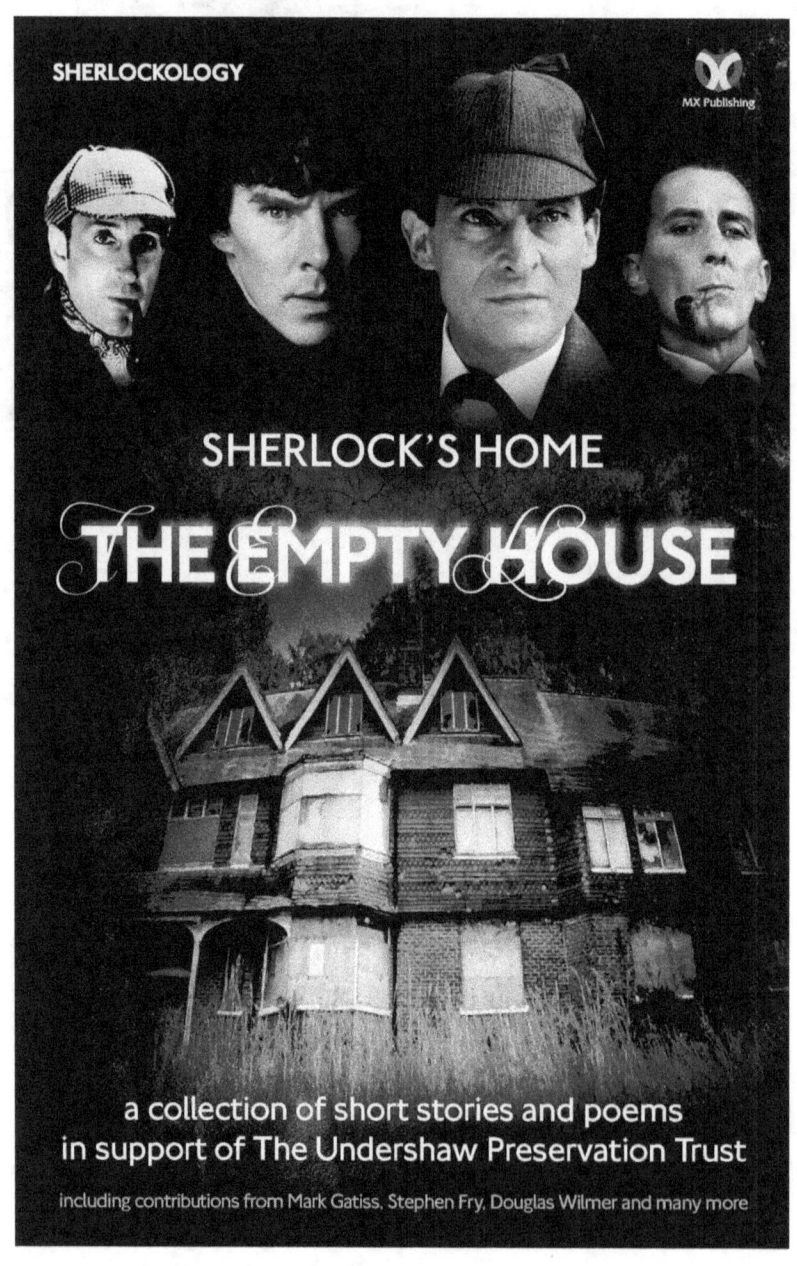

www.saveundershaw.com

www.mxpublishing.co.uk

The Curse of Sherlock Holmes – A Play Featuring Jeremy Brett

www.mxpublishing.co.uk

Benedict Cumberbatch, In Transition – A performance biography

www.mxpublishing.co.uk

Three hundred wonderful cartoons by Norman Schatell,
compiled by his son Glenn.

www.mxpublishing.co.uk

Also from MX Publishing – Over 100 new Sherlock Holmes stories.

Here are some of them………

www.mxpublishing.co.uk

www.ingramcontent.com/pod-product-compliance
Lightning Source LLC
Chambersburg PA
CBHW080716250626
47162CB00009B/2986

*9781780924243*